I0603221

WHEN LUCY CAME DOWN FROM THE
FERRIS WHEEL

When Lucy Came Down From the Ferris Wheel

VANESSA MCKAY

TeaTime Press

©Copyright 2021 by Vanessa McKay
All rights reserved. It is not legal to reproduce,
duplicate, or transmit any part of this document in either
electronic means or printed format. Recording of this
publication is strictly prohibited.
E-book ISBN: 978-0-6488713-6-1
Print-book ISBN: 978-0-6488713-7-8

Betrayal (noun) – the act of betraying someone or something or the fact of being betrayed: violation of a person's trust of confidence, of a moral standard, etc.
(The Merriam-Webster Dictionary)

RUNNING

"Harold, get Tom on the phone. She is at it again."

"Who is at what?" came her husband's voice from behind the newspaper.

"Lucy, you fool! I'll fetch the robe, you ring that husband of hers."

Lucy felt the soft, wet leaves beneath her feet. It was late afternoon, and the air was cool against her skin. She ran past the stone houses of Fremantle towards the Esplanade. Lucy could taste the salt air on her tongue. It was the taste of freedom.

Voices grew louder as she ran. She could just hear them behind the echo of the blood pumping in her ears. Fingers pointed at her goose-fleshed skin. Lucy leapt over the barrier like an athlete and began the climb up the support scaffolding of the Ferris wheel.

The grey-haired woman carrying a bathrobe broke apart the crowd that had gathered to watch. She called out, "Lucy, come down, my love. It is okay. She just forgets where she is sometimes. Help is coming. It's all going to be okay. Lucy!"

"Don't startle her," he said, placing a hand on her shoulder. "She will be okay, Gladys."

"I know. I only wish that she would remember to come to me when she needs help."

"She is not our Anna. You can't help everyone." Harold said.

Gladys turned and buried her face in the woollen cardigan he wore. He squeezed her.

"Just one time, Harold, one time I would like to be of some bloody use."

Police and ambulance officers arrived in a whirl of sirens and flashing lights. The crowd watched. A man climbed up the Ferris wheel. Gladys and Harold gave an officer Lucy's details. Someone on the ground called the hospital. A psyche patient was coming in. No one could contact her husband.

Across the Esplanade, Tom stood at the hotel room window, blowing cigarette smoke out into the cool October air. The shower had already stopped running. His dick hardened. He wanted to end this. He should do better. Be a better husband. The guilt ate at him. But he liked the sex. A lot.

"Lucy, hello, my name is Adam. I am here to help you get down safely. Will you take my hand?"

She looked into the distance. "I can see the works from here." She smiled.

"It is a beautiful view, but I am afraid you might fall. Please take my hand, and then I can enjoy the view with you," he said.

"Would you? Would you really sit and enjoy the view with me?"

"Sure, I will, if you promise to hold my hand. Then I will watch the sunset with you. Would that be okay, Lucy?"

She reached out and took hold of the hand he offered.

He tucked a blanket around her shoulders, and together they sat and watched the last few minutes of the sun going down.

DR SAM

"Lucy, do you know where you are?"

"I know you, Dr Sam," said Lucy.

"Yes, Lucy, you had another episode. Do you remember?" asked Dr Sam.

Lucy shook her head.

"Do you remember what happened yesterday?"

Lucy held her hand to her heart. "It hurts in here."

"Your heart?"

"No deeper, inside here." She pounded her chest with her fist. "In here. You can't fix this, Sam, not with all your talk, and it doesn't go away with all your pills. Tell them to let me sleep. I'm tired. If I sleep long enough, I can forget for a while."

"Not yet, Lucy. We need to know what happened yesterday."

"Where is Tom?"

"He will be here later. He has taken the kids to school."

"The kids?"

"Marty and Jonah."

"Yes, I know their names. I just wanted to know if you did after all this time."

"How much time?"

"Since we were at school, then since university, I think

you may know too much about me. I don't know that you should still be my doctor."

"Are you asking me to quit? Do you want me to refer you to someone else? I could, it just means you would have to start all over again. Is that what you want?"

"No, just make me sleep. I will talk to Tom later. I am tired now, please help me rest."

"Okay, Lucy, everything is fine. I will prescribe something and get the nurse to come along soon. We can talk about what happened yesterday later."

"Yes. Just not now. I don't want to talk."

TOM

"Tom, I told you, I don't know why she doesn't want to talk to you. I have told you everything she said. I am sorry she doesn't want to see you. Perhaps she is afraid of you?" said Sam.

"Afraid of me, what? Why?" said Tom.

"I don't know, but we are working on it. Why don't I come over tonight and cook you and the kids some dinner? Maybe a bottle of wine for after?"

"I do not think so, Sam. It's not right. I think it is best that we should stop seeing each other."

"No, I do not want to stop seeing you. It won't make Lucy better, it would just make you and me miserable." said Sam.

"Don't I get a say in this?" asked Tom.

"No. You know you want me. Do not fight it. We are good together," said Sam.

"It is just sex," said Tom. "I can live without it."

"I know that, of course, it is just sex." She hangs up the phone, then throws the receiver across the room.

LUCY

Lucy could feel the plastic-wrapped hospital mattress through the gap in her hospital robe. She counted the ninety-six foam tiles on the ceiling and wondered how she got here. *Where is Tom?* She thought back to yesterday morning—when he kissed her awake, it was early. He was dressed for work. Lucy wrapped her arms around his neck. She wanted to make love, feel his body on hers, replenishing her, making her feel. Anything. For him. Lucy knew what he wanted, but she felt dead inside, no desire, no lust, and she could not understand it. Why did she feel this way when she loved him so much?

Lucy reached for the buzzer and called the nurse.

"Good morning, Lucy," the nurse chirped into the room.

"Morning, I want to see my husband, please."

"Oh, he will be pleased. He seemed quite when Dr Sam instructed us to tell him you refused to see him."

"I didn't refuse to see him."

"Yesterday, your doctor said."

"No, I did not. Why would I do that?"

"Perhaps you are a little confused from your episode yesterday. No matter now. I will call him and tell him the good news."

"Thank you. Is Dr Sam here?"

"No, would you like me to call her?"

"No, thank you. I just want to see Tom."

Alone again, Lucy lay her back into the pillow, her focus was on the first tile, and it took her mind back to yesterday.

Tom woke her, kissed her, she held him, squeezed him, he pulled away. There was something in his eyes. Was it longing, pain, love?

After Tom had left for work she had showered in cold water, wanting the sharpness of the chill to wake her skin, to feel her skin, even as she rubbed herself red-raw with the loofah - nothing. Over breakfast, she listened to the chatter of her son and daughter.

"What's happening at school today?" she had asked them. She couldn't stabilize her attention for long enough to record the answer. Lucy had looked deep into their faces as they spoke. She heard the words they were saying, but she couldn't remember what they were. Not one. So, she had nodded and smiled. Her daughter saw it, that smile again, the one that didn't reach her eyes. She was only eight years old but knew when she was going to lose her mother for a while.

"Mum, I do not want to be late for school. Can we go now?" said Marty.

"I'm ready, sweetheart."

At the kiss and drop, she pressed a firm kiss on both their foreheads and watched them run up the school path until they disappeared into the bustling hive swarming to class.

An impatient mum eager to take her turn beeped

behind her. "Fuck the fuck up," Lucy had whispered into the rear-view mirror.

She took the long way home along the coast, past the Ferris wheel and up South street to her home. Lucy undressed at the front door before stepping inside. She was alone. It was a cool spring day. Sweat beaded on her skin.

"Google play radio, play anything louder please."

She went through to the kitchen, gathered up the breakfast dishes and took them outside to the green wheelie bin, dumped them in, and went upstairs to her bedroom. Stopping in front of the full-length wall mirror, she grabbed her rounded belly, squeezed the handful of overhang. *What is wrong with me?* Lucy ran her hands down the sides of her body, around her buttocks, alternating light feather touches with flesh squeezing; coming to her breasts, she watched herself in the mirror circle her right nipple, pinch it, take a handful of pliable breast and squeeze it. Her other hand wandered between her legs; a finger found her hole. She was wet but felt nothing, no longing, no wanting, no yearning.

The phone rang downstairs, and she climbed into bed. Lucy planted her face into the pillow that he slept on— nothing. *Is it him? Am I just not attracted to him anymore?* She took her rabbit from the back of her bedside table junk drawer, *guaranteed to please* the late-night ad had said. The machine whirred and rotated. She rubbed it between her legs, inserted it inside and ran through the motions, raising her hips, thrusting her hips back and forwards. She secured it upright with her hand and straddled it like a lover, suffocating her face in his pillow, visualizing him, breathing in his scent as she rammed herself hard on the machine until her legs tired. Nothing.

Lucy did not want to entertain the thought that Tom was at fault. She loved him and she had known they were meant to be together from the moment they met. She could not bring herself to place blame on him. They had met at a bachelor party where Lucy and her friend Sam were working as dancers to earn money during university —or at least that was the story she had told Tom. He never pressed her for more details, he was content without knowing the full truth.

She lay on the hospital bed thinking about the first time someone paid her for sex, an older business executive that smelt too much of aftershave. He took a blue pill when he arrived and licked her until he went hard. He kept asking her if he was good, then started telling her he was: "I am good, aren't I?" he said over and over. He was good. She closed her eyes so as not to see his lined face and greying hair between her legs; she came multiple times, and he applauded himself each time. "I am good", he would say over and over. He put his own condom on before he entered her. He was big and harder than she expected when he rammed himself home to climax, bringing her along for the ride. The best part was she got paid three hundred dollars for two hours of cunnilingus. They weren't all that easy, but Sam had been right. They were making good money while their classmates were sucking it up in the cafes.

The nurse put a cup of tea and a twin packet of biscuits on the bedside table.

"Everything alright, dear? Your husband will be in later this afternoon. He sounds lovely. He is very concerned and asked me to contact Dr Sam as soon as you are ready to talk. Are you in any pain? You must feel sad. It's okay, dear, you are not alone, lots of women suffer from post-natal depression. It can rear its nasty head at any time and bite you in the arse. Good job you have that doctor friend of yours; She is so concerned for you, asking that I give you the medicine she prescribed, and not what the doctors here prescribe. Not sure what to do, so I am waiting until the registrar comes through, can't be too careful, and we do not want a mix up of medications. There, I will fix your pillow. How's your tea, it's bushels! There, there, I will be back soon."

"Thank you," Lucy said as the nurse bustled her way out of the door.

The door closed, the room returned to quiet, and she focused on tile number two. After the rabbit, she had slept naked amongst the rumpled sheets. A stream of sunlight entered through the window, blinding her and instantly triggering a throbbing headache. She had wandered downstairs and poured herself a glass of wine and put some steaks in the sink to thaw. She took a couple of pills, turned the stereo up, and laid on the sofa. The radio DJ read some advertisement for erectile disorder pills, and she ran through the slide show of her ex-lovers, both on and off the job. She left out the few that disgusted her; the one that did not shower, the one that repeatedly tried to put his slug tongue into her mouth; the boy that fucked her in the back seat of his father's car and preceded to tell the world that he took her cherry. Lucy never had the heart to tell him it was long gone.

Those nights with Sam, pills, drinks and playing around; they were something, and she felt in the moment that she must be gay. It was too good, it made her feel too alive, too real, it was ecstasy. But Sam had convinced her it was just the pills and drinks, that nothing beat dick, and they both knew it. Lucy hadn't been so sure. She had felt she was falling in love. Sam, the touch of her soft hands on her skin, her breasts in her mouth, the oral, the fucking with a strap on, was all different from anything she had experienced before. She wanted more of her, of Sam.

Alone on the couch, her hand slipped between her legs, circled her slits, rubbed on her sweet spot, but this too was all for nothing even as she squeezed a breast to bruising, nothing. It hurt, but she felt nothing like pleasure in touch, in fantasy. Nothing could stir her. She took the bottle and refilled the wine glass.

Damn you, Sam, not even you can turn me on. She could have been content with only Sam. But Sam stopped playing. Sam betrayed her. She was more than Lucy's best friend, roommate and lover, she was Lucy's link to the agent that fed them the work. After a month of not hearing from her, Lucy had deleted Sam's number from her phone.

She had focused her attentions on Tom, was careful with her money, and pretended to herself that Sam was a fling and Tom was the real thing. In bed she could forget about everyone else. There was only them in the universe. Tom and Lucy fell in love so quickly and lusted so hotly that the world around them melted away.

Lucy poured another wine. Her chest was pounding. The sound of her blood rushing through her ears grew louder. Lucy's head hurt. When she closed her eyes, the room spun. She could see the colours through her closed lids, filling up the room. *It must be time*, she thought, *the children will finish school soon, I have to go now.*

The leaves were wet beneath her, before the bitumen bit sharply on the soles of her soft, groomed feet. She smelt the salt on the air and had to be near it, to see the sun kiss the ocean, so she ran. Past the beeping horns, the yells, someone clapping, not far away, someone whistled. The blood rushing through her ears was deafening, her breasts bounced, the tummy her kids made jiggled up and down, she felt sweat and maybe a little wee trickle down her inner thigh. She ran steadily; it was five kilometres to where she had to be. She paced herself. She should have rung Tom, but it was too late now. He could collect the kids. It was too late now. *I do not want him to see me like this.* The rising sweat clamped her hair to her face. She could not stop running now. It was too close. She could feel her breath catch in the back of her throat. She recalled what her yoga instructor told her: *come back to your breath, when all is gone, your mind, your train of thought, your patience, come back to your breath.*

Lucy had lost everything in this moment. Tom was going to take the children away, Sam would lock her up, her job gone. None of that mattered, she was dead inside, she felt nothing.

Lucy could see the giant wheel waiting to lift her up. There was a crowd, people laughing, some asking her if she was okay, others looked away. She heard her name called in the distance as she jumped the barrier to gasps and began climbing up the scaffolding frame of the Ferris wheel. Lucy heard her name being called again, a shrill desperate voice. There were sirens, then the voices below hushed. All she could hear was the sound of her breath and her blood beating in her ears.

TOM

Tom stood by her bed. "Lucy?" He placed a flower arrangement on the tray table it was made up of brightly coloured gerberas and native leaves. She wanted roses.

"Tom, did you know that Sam and I had a lesbian thing back at University?"

"Lucy." Tom said.

"Did you? Did I tell you?"

"Lucy, what are you trying to do?"

"Feel. Maybe if you react, if I can make you feel, then I will feel something. Tom, I am so tired of this life." Lucy said.

"Is that why you ran? Naked?" asked Tom.

"Yes."

"And what did you feel? What did you feel running naked down our street past our neighbour's houses and through Fremantle with old Gladys chasing you with a kimono robe she keeps by the door just for you?" Tom asked.

"I do not know, I don't feel. Anything. You are right to be angry, but I do not even feel remorse, concern, excitement, or embarrassment. Just nothing, it is not normal, what is wrong with me?" She lays back into her pillows.

"Have you been taking your medication? Honestly?

Sam says that you can't be taking it all the time and keep having these relapses."

"I am taking it, exactly as prescribed."

"And the wine?" asked Tom. He sits in the visitors chair, his hands on his knees.

"The wine is to stop me. Tablets and alcohol are supposed to make you drowsy, but they didn't. If they had, the worst case scenario is that you would have found me naked and drunk on the couch."

"That would have been better. You made the news this time. I don't know what your mum is going to say. Then again she may not know it is you because your face, amongst other things is pixelated on the footage."

"I am sorry. You are mad at me."

"I am not mad. Scared, but not mad. You haven't been the same since the twins were born. Sam can't explain why it is taking you so long to recover." He leans towards the bed and takes her hand.

"Do you trust Sam?" asked Lucy. She turns on her side to face him.

"She is your best friend. What are you saying?"

"I don't know, but what if maybe she is wrong? Please get me admitted with a new doctor, just this once, please. Sam was here earlier, and the nurses are not too fond of her. One said that there had been trouble in the past with her prescribing the wrong medication and she refused to listen to the other doctors even when she was wrong. She said my mix was a little off."

"Sam said she is trying something new, maybe she is ahead of the doctors here," said Tom.

"Yes, maybe, and maybe she is using me as a guinea pig. Whatever her reason, it still isn't working. Please."

"Of course, if you think it will help, I will ask Sam to recommend someone." Tom said.

"No, say nothing to Sam. Please."

"Won't that look a little strange?"

"Look, get me discharged, let me go to mum's and see a doctor down there, just tell Sam I am getting out of town for a while."

"Okay, I will come with you."

"No, stay here with the kids."

"I want to come with you, talk to your mum, and make sure that you are being well taken care of. We can take the kids over the weekend, then they can come back with me. I can shuffle things around at work and take care of them. This could be good for you, Lucy."

"The kids, do they know?"

"Well, considering you ran right past their school, amazingly no. I told them you were resting for a few days."

"I am sorry, Tom, I know that these few years have been hard on you. I love you. With all my heart, I love you. I am not sure why you put up with me."

"I did not marry you for sex. A good-looking guy like me can get that anywhere." He smiled and winked at her. "I married you because I love who you are, my Lucy. This is not your fault, and I am sorry I come across as being short-tempered, but it truly is because I am worried about you. One of these days something bad is going to happen to you, and I won't be there. Let's do this. I will call your mother and arrange things there and ring Sam and tell her you are coming home. Should I just tell her you forgot to take a pill?"

"Yes, but I didn't, Tom, I take all my pills, you must believe me."

He kissed her on the forehead. "I will arrange everything and come back for you."

AT THE BAR

Lucy came home from work one Tuesday night, after working a bad stag party. The rule was that the punters could touch, fondle her breasts and rub her snatch for a tip, but the boys this night took it way too far. Near the end they had collectively decided that they had paid enough and she was theirs.

Sam was out the back giving head for redbacks while six others had Lucy jammed into a corner of the bar. The men took turns raping her. The others cheered the penetrator while someone poured laybacks down her throat to muffle her protests. When they were done, the men left the bar without looking back to where she was. Their semen pooled down her legs and onto the floor, liquor stuck to her hair and drenched her skimpy costume. They left Lucy pathetic and stained, propped up against the bar. Her legs squelched as she brought them together. She was grateful the bar was empty; the regular staff had left long ago, her humiliation was secret. She called out for Sam, but nothing. In the locker rooms she showered with hand soap from the dispenser, dried herself with paper towels, got dressed, and left through the staff door.

On her way to her car, she saw Sam's purple hatchback rocking back and forth, windows steamed, and two men waiting their turn outside.

At home Lucy tried to quietly slip in through the carport door. Her mum was sitting at the kitchen table, flipping through the pages of a magazine.

"How was work love, would you like a cup of tea?"

"Yes please Mum, I will just run upstairs to shower. A keg blew on me." Grateful her mum did not look up from the magazine, Lucy ran up the stairs to the bathroom. In the shower she scrubbed herself sore under the scalding water.

When Lucy joined her mum at the kitchen table, a cup of tea was waiting for her with a digestive biscuit on the side.

"Thanks, Mum, but you didn't have to wait up. You must be tired from looking after Dad all day," said Lucy.

"I am okay, Lucy. I want to talk to you, and I do not want you to take it the wrong way. I know you are not working at the university tavern, that you have been working as a skimpy, and I know it is none of my business. You are twenty-one, a young adult woman, but you are still my daughter and I will wait up a million sunrises to make sure that you are home safe."

"Mum..." There were tears in her eyes.

"Now, Lucy, I love you, and yes, it is true that I won't always agree with your choices, but there probably is not much wrong with flashing a bit of boob and arse to make some money. I do not know where you get the courage from. Are you okay?"

Lucy threw her arms around her mother's neck. "I love you. Mum. I am alright, a little embarrassed. I did not want you to be ashamed of me. How did you find out?"

"Sam, she told me. It was like she was trying to shock me. I just acted like I knew already and thought it best that you knew I knew, then you would never have to keep secrets from me. You two have been friends for so long it surprises me. I thought when you went to university you would go your own way, but she always seems to follow you. Remember when she had you take the blame for shoplifting because her mum refused to buy her shoes for school? If you ask me, you have always been a better friend to her than she deserved. There she goes again, just today dobbing you in again as if you were twelve years old."

"Mum, I know, but she has always had it harder than me. I could say no, couldn't I, but I just do not have the heart. There is always a story, a time, and reason," said Lucy.

"Do not let her use you love, you are both adults now and you do not need to stay in a destructive friendship. It's up to you. I will always love you either way. Just remember that while life wasn't meant to be easy, it wasn't meant to be a torturous journey either."

"I love you, Mum, and I know you are right. I just do not know how to get away from her. Sam is quite persuasive." Lucy stood up and hugged her mum tight, and her mum squeezed back like she did as a child and planted a mother's kiss on her forehead. Lucy felt twelve again.

"Get some rest, my beautiful."

"You too." Lucy said.

"I will, I just have to check on your father."

"Let me, Mum, I haven't seen him all day." Lucy said.

"Okay, thanks, love, just check his drip is flowing and I will have that shower I have been waiting for."

"Sorry, Mum." Lucy said.

"Say no more, beautiful girl."

Lucy paused at the entrance of her father's home hospital room. He was in the end stages of pancreatic cancer. He came home to spend what time he had left with his family.

Oscar the retriever wagged his tail lazily as she entered the room, and she bent to scratch his soft, golden fur. There was a small, wrought-iron daybed that was barely big enough for an adult next to the hospital bed where her mum spent every night listening to her husband's breaths. He would be gone any day now. Lucy checked her father's drip was still pushing saline and much-needed morphine into his system. She counted the drips and stroked the hair from his forehead.

She looks to the big Chesterfield sofa chair in the room's corner, flanked on either side by bookcases running the length of the wall. She once sat on her father's knee while he read to her, and later when he taught her to read the tales of Christopher Robin and Pooh.

"How are you doing, Dad? Are you comfortable? Maybe we could talk in the morning, or I could read to you? The way you did for me when I was little. We miss you, Dad." She kissed his forehead. "I love you." Just before she left the room, the dog slid back onto his bed, having relieved himself. "Dad, I am sorry if I ever let you down. I will do better, Dad, I promise. Good night."

Lying now on her own hospital bed, she wondered,

Why did Sam tell her mum? They agreed to keep it between them, sure what they were doing was risky, and sometimes she regretted agreeing to do it, but overall, it was good. She had made good money and even enjoyed it sometimes. There was something wrong. She couldn't work it out with her fuzzy head.

FUNERAL

The rain fell heavily throughout the day. Lucy and her mum walked dutifully behind the casket from the church at Karrakatta to the crematorium. On the surface her mother had appeared stoic, yet Lucy could feel her hand shaking in her own. Two hundred and eighty-three people paid their respects that day. Not one of them had shown up to see him after the diagnosis.

When the wake was over and the house was clearing, Lucy put a cup of tea in front of her mum and joined her at the kitchen table.

"I am glad that they have all gone, the hypocrites. Where were they through the illness? They only had to sit with him. He needed company, to talk, to feel normal. He was so lonely."

"I'm sorry, Mum, I could have done more." Lucy said.

"Lucy, you did what could you do. It was good enough that you moved back home. Dad loved knowing that you were close. He worried about me right until the end. He kept saying, "Lucy's home," and he smiled."

"Thank you, Mum. I am glad that I got to spend time with him and with you. I will stay as long as you need me." Lucy said.

"No, really, there is no need. You get out into the world and live your life again. I will always miss your dad, whether you are here or not, but I do not want you to miss out on your life because of me, and your dad wouldn't want you to either."

"Mum, I do not want to leave you alone in this big house. It doesn't seem right." Lucy said.

"Lucy, I am not a child, dear, I will be okay. Besides, I may sell the house."

"Sell the house?" asked Lucy.

"Yes, it is too big, and well, I am surrounded by memories of your dad. He was the love of life, but I have no intention of spending the rest of mine in a shrine."

"Where will you go?" asked Lucy.

"I do not know, but before the diagnosis, we talked about getting one of those camper trailers and driving, anywhere that took our fancy. We were going to go off and see Australia, maybe even hop a continent. Have an adventure. When Dad's ready, I will take him with me."

"What do you mean when Dad is ready?" asked Lucy.

"Oh my god, your face, Lucy. I know, for a second there, you thought I was being delusional. I meant when they give his ashes to me. I could take him along. Like we planned."

"Yes, I thought that is what you meant." Lucy said.

"Have another cup of tea dear, you look pale."

TOM

"What is this talk about Lucy being discharged from hospital? I am her doctor and I decide what is in her best interests." Sam stood at Tom's door.

He saw the bottle of wine in her hand and smiled dryly. "I told you that this is not a good time, Sam, I am just putting the kids to bed."

"No, you are not, Lucy told me they are both at your parent's house. We are alone, so how about I make us something to eat while you open the wine?"

"I do not think so, Sam," said Tom.

"What do you mean, you do not think so? Do you have someone else here?" Sam pushed past him into the foyer, dumped her keys, her coat, her bag, and the wine on the hall table like this was her own house and went from room to room on a manhunt.

Tom followed behind helplessly. "What do you think you are doing? I did not invite you in, Sam, I asked you to go home."

"That is not what you told me yesterday when my lips were around your dick!"

"Sam, go. Please." said Tom.

She softened her gaze and fingered the buttons on his shirt. "Really? Do you want me to go home? I pass the hospital, and maybe I could call in on Lucy to let her know we were catching up while she was having a breakdown. Let her know we like to catch up, how fucking me has saved your pathetic excuse for a marriage, I am doing her a favour, she is frigid, and you know how hot I can be." Sam said.

"Sam, it is over. I truly just want to do what I can to help Lucy, to get her home and to get her life back, the way it was before the post-natal depression." Tom said.

"She will never come back. She has gone too far. I may even have to have her committed. Permanently." Sam said.

"You wouldn't do that, you are supposed to be her friend." Tom said.

"Want to test me? I am also your lover. How do think this will look?" Sam asked.

"How, indeed? I can report you for misconduct. You swore an oath, not me, you have a doctor-patient relationship with my wife, and you seduced me." Tom said.

"Did I? Or did I call to see you, concerned for your welfare, for Lucy and the grave decision you made in packing her off to her mother in Albany, and you..." Sam stopped.

"I what? What lies will you tell?" Tom asked.

She pressed her mouth hard onto his, her left hand squeezed his cock as her right hand worked its way into his trousers. He tried to move away, but she had him. He was swept up in hating her and lusting after her. She was sexy, even with her ugly nature. Her mouth was on him; his hand grabbed the back of her head, scrunching a fistful of hair, her hands pulled along the length of his legs, and with her mouth working his cock he made his way to lying there on the marble tiles of their entrance floor. He closed his eyes, so he didn't have to watch. She straddled him, taking him in one slick blow. Tom didn't hold back, he came and willed himself limp in minutes.

She stood over him. "Do you honestly believe that I can't keep Lucy in that hospital for as long as I want?" Sam asked.

"Why don't you let her go to her mother's? She will be away, my parents could take care of the children, and we could spend some time together, see if our relationship has a future." Tom said.

"A future? You have been fucking me for eight years, all the time Lucy has been sick, do you think you are being a good husband?" Sam asked.

"You seduced me, you wanted me..."

"No. Tom, you wanted, and you took from me. I was the one trying to do right. If you fucked me, then you wouldn't have to go anywhere else and Lucy wouldn't lose her husband."

"That is not how I remember it." Tom said.

"It's okay, Tom, you will soon know what I mean," said Sam, collecting her things and leaving him alone.

He lay on the floor, his hands over his limp dick, feeling pathetic. His heart raced as he put his pants back on and raced from the house. At the hospital he found Lucy was alone, staring at the tiles on the ceiling.

LUCY

"Lucy, what are you up to?" asked Tom, entering her room.

"Three, number three," said Lucy.

He looked up to where she was staring. "Is everything okay?" Tom asked.

"Yes, just running shit through my brain, trying to work things out. Trying to figure out how I got here." Lucy said.

"How is it going?" He kissed her forehead.

"I need to get away, Tom. Please say that I can go to Mum's and stay for a while, see someone down there, and maybe you could bring the kids down on the weekend.

The house she is watching has loads of space..." Lucy said.

"Sounds like you have been talking to your mum already." Tom said.

"Yes, I have, I feel like there is something that we are missing, that I am missing a trigger, something out of my control. You know that I have read everything that I can get my hands on for post-natal depression, and so much doesn't add up." Lucy said.

"Yes, I know, I know. Sam doesn't think you should go away."

"Tom, I am certain that Sam is the problem."

"What? Do you think Sam is making you sick?"

"She is not making me better. Please say I can go. I need you to sign me out into your care."

"Of course, I will do it first thing in the morning." Tom said.

"No, Tom, do it now, then take me straight to my mother's, please. I can't go home. She will find me." Lucy said.

"She knows that you are going to your mother's." Tom said.

"Yes, but she doesn't know where my mother is now," said Lucy.

"I, um, may have mentioned Albany, I am not sure, but anyway, it is a big enough place to get lost in. Besides, I doubt she will chase you anywhere, she is just worried for you and trying to help you, I'm sure," said Tom.

"Maybe. If they tell me the same thing there then yes, Sam is right, I am nuts, and we should get a divorce."

"Who said anything about getting a divorce?"

"Sam. In my last session, she said that I was being unfair to you. It was cruel to trap a man in a frigid, sterile relationship, that you deserved so much better, a full life, that I couldn't give you."

Tom sat on the edge of her bed he pulled her to him, hid his face in her blonde hair. "Lucy, you are my wife, my life, and my everything. I will never leave you. I will always love you, no matter what," said Tom.

"I know, I am just trying to be fair to you," said Lucy.

"You are honey. I am going to sort out the discharge and get you out of here."

Without stopping for a change of clothes, they took to Albany highway and arrived at Isabel's house in the early hours of Wednesday morning. The door swung open as the car pulled into the drive.

"Typical early riser." Tom smiled.

Lucy leapt out the car the second it stopped and ran up the drive to hug her mum. Izzy squeezed her daughter tight. "It is going to be okay, Lucy, come inside, the pair of you. I have made some breakfast for you both."

"Thanks, Izzy, I am starving," said Tom.

"I thought you might be Tom. Thanks for driving my daughter home. Don't worry, we will sort everything out here with no interference. I have the name of a good doctor over in Mt Barker. Thinking that Sam is possessive enough of Lucy's care to put the kybosh on any doctor treating here without prejudice, but she wouldn't think about infecting the ones out of town."

"Good thinking, Mum." Lucy said.

After a breakfast of pancakes and fruit muffins, Lucy headed upstairs for a shower and a change of clothes. She was the same size as her mum, so she gratefully took up the offer to change out of the hospital gowns they discharged her in.

"Sam called me last night, after she left you. She told me that you two were having an affair, that it was going on for a long time, and last night she tried to end it and you refused and forced yourself onto her." Isabel said.

"What, forced myself onto her?"

"She is saying that you raped her."

"No, that is not what happened at all. Yes, regretfully,

we were having an affair, I wish I could say that was a lie, but I told her that was over last night. She threatened to commit Lucy forever, warned me not to bring her here, and then forced herself on me. I was afraid of what she would do to Lucy. I am sorry. So sorry, I tried to end it, I did not rape her, Izzy, please believe me."

"I do, Tom. I have known Sam since she was eight years old, and she has always been a manipulative bitch. She told me she has gone to the police, had a rape kit done, but wouldn't be pressing charges because she is worried about what the effect would be on Lucy, but her telling me is a threat of what she will do if we take Lucy away from her care. Why Tom? What is it she wants?"

"I think she wants to be my Lucy," said Tom.

"Sounds about right. If we are right, and she has been making Lucy sick for all these years under the guise of helping her, what else is she capable of?" said Isabel.

"I should stay here, keep you both safe." Tom said.

"No, we are okay. I have a friend with a gun across the street with a sharp eye and a nosy disposition. Besides, she doesn't know where I live. This is a new house-sitting gig. So, how could she? You should get home, act normal, get a nanny cam or two set up—these houses use them all the time to check up on their pets and sitters. If what happened last night happens again, and it just might, you will have evidence that she threw herself at you and not the other way around."

"That is a good idea. What should I tell Lucy?"

"Tell Lucy about what?" Lucy entered the room.

"Tom was just talking about the kids being at his

parents. He is worried that you might not think it is a good idea, that they are a little different." She winked at Tom.

"I am afraid, Mum, that I really have little say as to what Tom has to do to keep things together up in Fremantle. If it is easier to have the kids with his parents, what is the worst that can happen? Going to church never killed anyone. Besides, they could use a little fire-and-brimstone discipline, learn about what happened back in Tom senior's day, walking five miles to school in the ice and sleet and all the rest."

"Hey, that is my upbringing you are making fun of." Tom stood and moved around the table to hug Lucy. "I should get back. I still need to get into work this morning."

"Should I pack you some food?" Isabel said.

"No thank you, Izzy, I am full, thank you." He let go of Lucy and hugged his mother-in-law.

She patted his back and told him that everything was going to be okay.

TOM

Tired from driving through the night, Tom pulled into his driveway without seeing the red sports car parked out the front of his house. She was sitting on the porch swing, foot tapping, reading something on her phone, when he finally noticed her.

"What are you doing here?" he asked.

"What do you mean, what am I doing here? Where is my patient?"

"You mean where is my wife?"

"They discharged her into your care last night. I expect to see her in your care, yet somehow you are alone. Where is she? Do I have to call for a search? Call the police to search? Find her and bring her back to hospital?"

"No, I transferred her care to a very responsible person, so you can just leave us alone."

"Do you mean that mother of hers? The drunkard, hippy, stoner, yoga-loving gypsy woman with no fixed address?"

"I do not understand why you don't want the best for Lucy; it's like you are trying to keep her sick."

"How dare you! Is that what you think is happening here? Maybe it is you trying to keep her sick, imagine how bad she will feel, how far off the rails she will go when she finds out that you have been fucking her best friend!"

"You are not her best friend, you have done nothing but sabotage Lucy her entire life."

"Really? I did not force her to be an escort, a skimpy, a stripper; I did not force her to have a lesbian affair or to marry you; and if I remember rightly, I did not force you into fucking me either. You look shocked, didn't you know your precious Lucy's sordid secrets? Do you think that being a lesbian is why she can't stand your beautiful cock?"

She reached forward to cup his manhood, but he blocked her hand away.

"Stay away from us. I do not want to see you again, I do not want you to come anywhere near me or my family every again." Tom yelled.

"Really, do you think you can keep me away? One phone call and Lucy is back in Belmont and under my care." Sam smiled.

"Leave us alone." Tom pushed past her through to the front door, closed it behind him, then he slid to the ground on the inside of the door.

His breath still short, he phoned Izzy on his mobile. "Get Lucy to hospital now, get her under a doctor's care now. Sam was just here, and she threatened to have Lucy brought back to hospital here by the police."

"What the fuck is that cow up to? You need to get a restraining order today Tom, keep her away from you and your family." Izzy said.

Without stopping to shower, Tom headed to Fremantle police station and stood in front of the same officer that saw Sam the day before.

"I need a restraining order please," he said to the officer across the counter.

"Do you believe that someone is posing a danger to yourself or your family, sir?"

"Yes, I do. She was my wife's doctor, friend, then doctor. We believe she is a danger, she means to hurt my wife."

"Is your wife in physical danger, sir?"

"No, I do not think so. She doesn't know where my wife is but she keeps turning up at my house, threatening me, threatening her."

"This all sounds a little sticks and stones, sir."

"Maybe I am not explaining this properly. She hasn't done anything we can prove yet, but that doesn't mean she won't or that she hasn't. This woman is mentally unstable." Tom said.

"Sir, we can't do too much on the chance that someone might do something. Okay, here is what we can do, we can make a report then if the harassment persists, we can send someone to talk to her."

"Thank you, that may help." Tom said.

The officer rolled her eyes, unconvinced that anything was going on other than a parting of ways and collected a form from under the desk.

"Name, please."

"Tom Ballard."

"Address."

"29 Adelaide Terrace, Fremantle."

"Hang on, what is the name of the person you are placing a complaint against?"

"Sam Halong."

"Sir, take a seat, I need to ask my super something."

"Really? Is everything okay?" Tom sensed something might be up.

"Please take a seat, sir."

Tom sat down on the wooden bench along the back wall, wiped his brow, and stood up to read the wanted notices on the wall behind him.

"Mr Ballard." A voice beside him introduced himself as Sergeant Leopold. "Can you come with me, please, I would like to ask you a few questions."

"Sure." Tom shrugged and followed the sergeant past the staff only door and along the corridor to a small, dank room.

"Take a seat, please, sir."

Tom did as instructed. "What is this all about?"

"Well." The sergeant sat down across the table from Tom, opened his notebook, and took out a pen. "It appears you are trying to take out a restraining order on a young lady named Sam Halong I have problem accepting your claim that you are in danger. Ms Halong was here yesterday, accusing you of rape, she was unsure whether she wanted to press charges because of the close family connection and a fear of how you would respond. Now today you are here asking for a restraining order against her. I have to ask, is it to stop your victim talking to your wife?"

"No, you do not understand. She seduced me, she seduced and coerced me for years, and every time I tried to stop she would threaten to tell my wife. This would destroy her. She is fragile enough. Sam is Lucy's doctor. Lucy is my wife, the Ferris wheel streaker?"

"Oh, that Lucy."

"Yes."

"Where is Lucy now?" asked Sergeant Leopold.

"I took her to mother's in Albany last night. Her mother is taking her to see a doctor today for assessment and returned to care if needed."

"What is wrong with your wife?"

"She suffered post-natal depression after the birth of our twins. They are eight years old, but she hasn't recovered. Sam was her doctor from the start. We are thinking now that was a mistake."

"Who is we?"

"Myself, Lucy and Isabel, her mother." Tom said.

"You understand I need to speak to them at some point? There are no charges against you yet. However, if what you are saying is correct, her aim could be to destroy you."

"That is what I am afraid of." Tom said.

THE FAT MAN

The day after the wake, her mum had rung a real estate agent to put the family home on the market. They set the price low, and it sold in weeks. Lucy and Izzy had a month to clear out a lifetime of belongings, memories, and cluttered drawers.

Izzy then bought a Winnebago, and Lucy moved in with Sam to share her Applecross apartment. One room, one bed, and a lot of late nights. The pair spent summer nights watching sunsets and drinking wine from a box by the Swan River. They were both at university, and the study load alone put pressure on them both. They worked their skimpy jobs to pay the bills, hibernated, studied, and explored their relationship.

It was during this time that Lucy was sure she was gay. It would likely affect her chances of teaching in a Catholic school like the one she went to, but it did not matter. Lucy was prepared to throw her childhood aspirations aside for love.

Sam would sometimes record their lovemaking sessions; she said it turned her on to be watched. Lucy did not care. She wanted Sam to be turned on, to love her and desire her, and she would do anything to please her.

It was a wet summer's night when Lucy was sitting alone drinking wine on the balcony of their little apartment overlooking the river. Startled from her daydream by Sam calling her name.

"Lucy, come inside, I want you to meet someone."

Lucy entered the house through the kitchen window to find Sam standing with her arm around a bearded man. He wore a flannelette shirt and ill-fitting leather pants. Tattoos on his arms and hands, a red bandanna on his head. He held a six-pack of beer in one hand and a dog leash in the other.

"This is Fred," said Sam.

"Ged," he corrected her.

"Does it matter?" Sam asked.

"Yes," he replied. "You promised you would take care of me, the least you could do is remember my name, or is that an extra?" He squeezed her behind as she pulled away.

"This is Lucy. I told you all about Lucy and how she likes it. Lucy will not disappoint you, I am sure."

"Sam, what is this?" asked Lucy.

"Customer, Luce. Things have been quiet lately, so I thought I would go out and get us some."

"Can I speak to you in the kitchen, privately?" Lucy growled.

"We will get this sorted and be right back," Sam said to Ged.

"I do not want this to be weird, I thought you were a professional, maybe I should go," said Ged.

"No, you stay right there, you will get what I promised you, and I will be here to see it." Sam joined Lucy in the kitchenette.

"What the fuck is this?" asked Lucy.

"You are going to do what he tells you, baby, and I am going to film you and watch. He is going to pay us five hundred dollars. It is an excellent offer, and all he wants you to do is let him fuck you while you are wearing the collar."

"A dog collar. What for?"

"Why not?"

"If it is so easy, why don't you do it, Sam?"

"I would, but I started my period, and he is squeamish. Come on, Lucy, you know we could use the money."

"That is all I have to do? Can we make him shower first?"

"Really, Lucy, you want that in our bathroom?"

"You want *that* to fuck me, to be inside of me?"

"Come on, Lucy, stop being such a whingy fart, when you are done I will go out and get us some Chinese take away and wine while you soak your pussy in a bubble bath, then I will reminded you why you like to fuck me better."

"I know why I like to fuck you..."

Sam stopped her words with her mouth, her hand on her breasts, tongues touching.

"Well, if that is what you prefer ladies, why don't we have a threesome?" said Ged.

"No, that's not happening, Ted. Lucy is your fuck, and I will be your camera gal as promised."

"Can you at least take your clothes off?" asked Ged.

"Sure, for a hundred more." said Sam.

"Deal."

Lucy laid out across the crinkled bed, messed up from

the morning's lovemaking. She let the man put the thick, spiked collar around her neck and secure it snugly. Ged tied the leash to the top of the bed. He ran his nose from the centre of her breasts towards her cunt, and instinctively she raised her hips to meet him, but he pulled away.

"Where is that friend of yours with the camera?"

Sam entered the room.

"What the fuck! You still have your clothes on."

"Yes, I do, I thought it would be nice for Lucy to watch me undress."

"Me first." The man pushed his jeans to the floor, letting his insignificant cock bounce out; removed his shirt to reveal his rounded, pale belly and man boobs; the smell of his stale sweat filled the air.

Lucy watched Sam lift her t-shirt up over her head; she was braless, her breasts bounced softly with the movement. She slid down her denim shorts and pulled her lace panties down to her ankles.

"You lied," Lucy gasped.

Sam winked. "I thought you would enjoy this more than I would. Ready when you are, stud," said Sam.

Ged planted his soft, fat body on Lucy, forced a stinking beer kiss across her mouth, and pushed his slug tongue down her throat until she wanted to choke. He sounded like he was devouring a juicy, summer peach; he was slurping and moaning at the deliciousness of her. Sam zoomed closer with the camera.

The man straddled up on Lucy's chest, fumbled to find his little cock, and rubbed it on her breasts. He moved in further to push it into her mouth. She took it without thinking of protection. Everything about this man was wrong. He pulled out before he came and let his juice run onto breasts and face.

Before she had time to clean up, he flipped her over. The action tightened the collar around her neck. With one hand under her stomach the other hand penetrated her hard; it was uncomfortable, and she gasped.

"There, my little lesbo, you like that, let me see if I can get my fist inside you." He kept working hard at her with his stubby, tobacco-stained fingers. She pulled up her hip, trying to move away to lessen his thrusting, but he smacked her hard.

"Sam, do something, this is hurting," said Lucy.

Sam stayed quiet and kept filming.

The man pulled her up on to her knees. "Stay, whore."

Fingers, thumb, and palm were inside her now. He moved it around, searching like he has lost something. Lucy pleaded for Sam to stop him, but when she looked at her, she could see Sam had one hand on the camera, the other on her own pussy. The man was tugging at his little cock, willing it to go hard. With one hand still inside her, he flipped Lucy again, pulled his hand out of her cunt, and forced his limp cock into her mouth.

It relieved her to have him out of her burning hole and she hoped that if he came again, he would leave her alone. She watched Sam pleasuring herself, watching her, and for a moment it was okay, until the slap across her face.

"Watch me, slut, not your lesbian girlfriend. Her show is for me, not you, I paid for that just like I paid for you."

Her face stung, and she tasted blood in her mouth, and

he slapped her again. Next, he grabbed a handful of her breast, squeezed the nipple hard, and bit it down between his teeth. Lucy thought she heard Sam applaud before he slapped her again.

Her ears were ringing when he flipped her over and shunted her arse up to his cock, then shoved his little member into her arse. He gripped on her hair, pulling her head back as he thrusted into her, tightening the collar around her throat. Her head inched closer to the headboard, and when she was making contact with it, he thrusted her harder. Even with her hand held up for protection, it wasn't enough; he fucked her into concussion.

It was dark when she woke up. The sheets were soddened with cum, blood, and sweat. In the bathroom mirror she saw her face was swollen, black and blue. More had happened to her body after she passed out. She had welts across her spine; her vagina and arse bled.

In the hallway's light she ran her own bath and emptied the Epson salts into the running water. It hurt to sit down in the water. "Sam, are you here? You bitch, you better be back soon with wine!"

She must have fallen asleep; when she woke again, the water was cold. Lucy pulled the plug and stepped into the shower; using their shared loofah, she scrubbed her body, trying to get the man stench from her body. She went through several layers of strawberry body shop scrub and body wash. When she was done Lucy wrapped a towel around her sore body and went through the tiny apartment switching on the lights, hoping to find Sam.

Sam still wasn't there, so Lucy pulled the sheets from

the bed, loaded the washer, put on her pyjamas, and curled up on the couch. She slept until the morning sun shone through the calico curtains and warmed her face.

"Sam, are you here?"

She went to the bedroom. Sam wasn't there, and all her clothes had gone. Somewhere in the middle of the night Sam had left, she left Lucy.

Why did she ever forgive Sam? She broke her heart.

Months later when they ran into each other at the high school reunion. Sam approached Lucy like they were long-lost friends, but Lucy pulled back, still hurting. All this time, after being left for dead.

Sam didn't give up, she cornered her in the ladies and pushed her into a cubicle. "We need to talk." Sam said.

"We needed to talk when you fucked off. What the hell was that about, you bring that thing into our home and make me fuck him, you let him do fuck god knows what to me, and then you pack up all your slutty clothes and fuck off! Who does that shit?"

"I had an accident."

"Bullshit, Sam. Was that before or after you packed your shit up?"

"After, but I meant to come back. I was jealous, you loved that cock."

"I hated everything about it, including the two broken ribs, blood nose and vaginal tears he gave me. You took money for my pain. You didn't give a shit about me. You left me."

Sam pressed her mouth onto Lucy's, but Lucy was not

having any of it. She bit down hard. She could taste Sam's blood on her tongue, and she was glad.

"Lucy, I am sorry."

"You were right about one thing."

"What's that?"

"I am not a lesbian. Thanks to you, I never want to touch another cunt again."

"Can we be friends?"

"I do not think so. Friends do not set each other up that way." Lucy unlocked the cubicle.

"I will not give up that easily."

"Nothing you do is ever going to make me trust you again. We are through, Sam Halong."

"Lucy, I am not giving up on our friendship."

"You don't get it, do you? When you left me, and you left me, alone without an explanation, you took all your clothes without so much as a goodbye, an explanation—fuck, you even took the money that I slaved for, that I was beaten for."

"Beaten? Don't you think you are overreacting, Lucy?"

"Don't you think that you are missing the fucking point?"

"Which is?" asked Sam.

"You let a stranger hurt me. A stranger that you brought into our home, then you broke my heart by leaving me without a trace. No one knew what happened to you, no one knew where you were, you did not stay to check that I was okay, or to say that you were sorry."

"Well, didn't I just try to apologise?"

"Leave me alone, Sam." Lucy turned away towards the

vanity and looked at Sam through the glass. She looked confused and lunged at Lucy from behind, wrapping her arms around her waist.

"Please, Lucy, forgive me, I am so sorry for what I did. I do not deserve you as a friend. I love you, I can't go on without you. Please say we can be friends again. I need you in my life."

Sam felt Lucy's shoulders soften.

"Maybe," said Lucy as she pulled Sam's arms away and walked away.

The nurse chirped into the room, "How are we today, Miss Lucy? We have your medication and some water. A cup of tea will be along soon."

"Thank you. Why did I let Sam get back into my life?"

"Excuse me, miss?"

"Nothing, sorry, I am just thinking out loud."

"No worries, petal, we all do it."

THE REUNION

The morning after the reunion, Lucy received a friend request from Sam via her Facebook page. Two days later she accepted, and within weeks the two friends were meeting up for coffee, then dinner, then dancing. There were a few sleep overs, but they are no longer lovers.

Sam convinced Lucy to quit her job at the Stationery Factory to join her once more in some regular skimpy gigs. The money was good, but Lucy said from the outset that she wouldn't be going any further.

"Stop going on please, Lucy, you make me feel so bad about what I did," said Sam.

"You feel bad, how the fuck do you think I felt?" said Lucy.

"Please, Lucy, we are moving on, I do not want to talk about it anymore."

The conversation would always go in circles. Lucy didn't know what she wanted from Sam, but nothing Sam said would soothe her hurt. Sam would just get shitty and Lucy would apologise for bringing it up again, and they would continue on the same.

It was a rainy October night when Sam and Lucy were working a stag night at the South Perth Yacht Club.

"That is barely skimpy," Sam said when Lucy took off her coat.

"It is skimpy enough, and it is as far as I am going for a stag do," said Lucy.

"What is wrong with you, Lucy? These gigs are a great way to make to money. Here, take a pill and chillax. We are going to be cashed up tonight."

"What is it?" Lucy asked.

"Valium. Go on, take it," Sam said.

"No, I do not think so. I want my wits about me tonight. I do not feel safe at these things."

He saw her from across the room. Shaking her head made her hair bounce from side to side, and the maid's costume she wore showed off her curvaceous figure. She looked different from the other girls. She looked classy and yes, sexy. He watched her as she took drink orders, keeping her distance from the boys. She was untouchable. Different from the blonde in red lace pushing her tits into the guy's faces as she was serving the drinks, hand on her hip, laughing.

It was his turn to order. "Hi, my name is Tom. What are you doing here?"

"I am here to take your order, sir," said Lucy.

"You do not look like you want to be here," said Tom.

"Don't be silly, sir, of course I want to be here, to celebrate the last night of freedom for your friend."

"Sorry, you misunderstood me. You do not look like one of the usual girls that work here."

"Sorry, what do you mean, one of those girls?"

"Oh my god, I did not mean to offend you. I am sorry, but you are different from the girl over there." He gestured over to where Sam laid across the table and the boys were taking turns lifting shots from her cleavage.

"No, I am not like her. Thank you for noticing."

"You two friends?"

"Sort of. We have known each other since we were eight years old. On and off."

"I am guessing she got you into this gig."

"Yes, we are at university. Good-paying part-time jobs are hard to find. This is not the best job. My mum is not happy about it, but the money is good. I don't do the same things as Sam, and it still pays well."

"You look beautiful. What are you are you studying at university?"

"Teaching degree. Sam is going to be a psychologist."

"Really. You I understand, I can see you as a teacher, but Sam a doctor?"

She laughed. "Yes, but really, she is very smart."

"Can I walk you home? If that is not too old-fashioned."

"Sorry, I do not go home with customers. It is my personal rule."

"I did not mean to walk you home as in come in for coffee and stay for breakfast. I actually meant can I see you home safely, find out where you live, and maybe send you flowers and pester you for a dinner date, lunch date, any date really, just an opportunity to learn about the girl behind the brown eyes. Sorry, that was creepy. You must be asked out all the time," said Tom.

"Well actually no, that was one of the sweetest pickup lines I have heard. You still can't walk me home, but I would very much like you to call me and discuss a date."

"Really?"

"Pass me your phone."

He took his phone from his pocket and handed it to her. She saved her number in his contacts, and he immediately called her, relieved when he heard her voice on the message.

"When you are finished flirting, I could use some help," came Sam's voice from across the table.

"Sorry, Tom, I have to go."

"Can I help?"

"Depends. How do you look in a teddy?" Lucy smiled.

"No, he can't help," Sam interrupted. "But for ten bucks he can squeeze my tits." She presented her ample breasts to Tom, pressing them together with her hands on either side.

"No thanks." He walked away to join his friends at the pool table, winking at Lucy.

"Well, he was rude," said Sam.

"No, he wasn't, Sam. He was nice."

"Really? Then what is he doing in a place like this? He is just a perve like the rest of them."

"Celebrating his friend's upcoming wedding, Sam."

Tom called that night and left a message: "Hi, it is me, Tom. I am hoped this is not coming across wrong, but I really enjoyed meeting you tonight. I am sure you actually get hit on by guys all the time, but I can't stop thinking about you. Can I see you soon? Call me in the morning or afternoon or middle of the night. I look forward to hearing your voice again and getting to know you. But if I do not hear from you, I promise I am not some creepy stalker guy. I will leave you be and be grateful for getting to know even a little bit about Lucy."

Lucy replayed the message over and over until she found sleep.

DATING

The following day they had lunch at the Sail and Anchor in Fremantle, and late that night he walked her to the door of her apartment. Kissed her softly and bid her goodnight. They had dinner the next night, and the next, and so on, for weeks. Each night, he kissed her softly and left her at the door until the night that she finally invited him inside.

"Give me a minute." She left him in the lounge room.

He sat and waited, taking in the fresh clean decor, white on green, crisp and fresh like she was. Nothing out of place, a faint smell of sandalwood.

"This is a really nice place." Tom said.

"Thanks," Lucy called from the bedroom where she was smoothing ruffled covers and pushing laundry under the bed along with the thirteen outfits she had discarded this week.

Then she stood at the bedroom door.

"Can I get you a drink? Tea, coffee, wine?"

"Wine would be nice. How long have you lived here?"

"About a year now. I moved here after Sam and I split. We used to share a place."

"Did you two have a falling out?"

"You could say that I enjoy living on my own. It is

nice to have a place to myself." She passed him a glass of chardonnay.

He sipped as she sat down, watching how she floated down onto the couch.

"Lucy."

"Tom."

He leaned in and kissed her, wrapping one arm around her shoulder, the other holding his glass. His kisses were warm, soft, firm, intense, and safe. Lucy softened into his chest. She giggled, pulled slightly away, watching his eyes while they both put their wine glasses on the table and returned to each other to lose time, entwined in the other's arms.

"Tom, it has been a while since I have been with a man. Forgive me if I seem awkward."

He kissed her along her neckline, lifted her chin.

She stopped him, and they stared into each other's eyes.

"Let's go play in my room?" Lucy said.

She stood up, and he followed her lead; near the bed, she turns around to kiss him. Tom ran his hands through her hair, stopping at the buttons of her blouse. He undid one button at a time, revealing her pink lace bra and breast. He kissed the flesh of one and then the other through the lace.

She reached behind to unclip her bra, and he cupped her breasts in his hands as the lace fell to the floor. She unzipped the back of skirt and let it fall.

He took a step back, taking in her curves and tanned skin. Stepping out of her skirt, she moved forward, ran her hands up his shirt; his arms went up, and she lifted it over his head. With her arms around his waist, she pressed into his tight, toned masculine chest, breathed in this scent and reached for his belt buckle to drop his pants to the floor. They stopped at his ankles, and he performed that jig men do to get their shoes off, socks, then pants. He was hard as he stood there in front of her for the first time. Both only in their underpants he stepped to her, ran his hands through her hair to hold the back of her neck, kissed her, and together they make their way onto the bed.

Each fumbled at removing the last barriers between them. He was as eager to enter her as she was to have him, but he desperately wanted to savour this moment. This first time with Lucy would never happen again. There was only one first time.

He pulled away slightly.

"Let me kiss you."

He started at her mouth, soft, butterfly kisses. She wanted him to go deeper, to feel his tongue in her mouth, but she liked the teasing too. She wanted this to last. From her mouth, his lips caressed her face, eyelids, cheeks, jaw-bone, neck.

He was kissing more firmly now, her back arched towards him.

"Shh, slowly," he whispered, making his way to her breasts.

Taking one nipple gently between his teeth then the other, a deep ache for him built inside her as he went down zigzagging across her torso, her hips, and down the length of each newly waxed leg towards her feet.

He was off the bed and standing over her. "Turn over."

"NO!" She was too sharp in her reply and covered with, "I want to see your face."

"I would, with your permission, like to kiss every inch of your body from head to foot, if you would let me?"

His soothing voice brought her back to now. She turned for him, and gently he kissed up the length of each of her legs, along her buttocks, and she can feel her face relaxing as he zig-zagged his way across her spine and her shoulders, coming to rest on the bed alongside her.

"I knew it," he said.

"Knew what?"

"That you are the most beautiful girl in the world. There is no way a girl like you would want a fool like me. I am just going to have to be content to be your plaything until your real man comes along."

"What are you talking about?"

"You are beautiful. I do not deserve to be with a girl like you."

She kissed him passionately, and he returned in kind. "Stop fishing for compliments and take me."

FACE MASK

Lucy's mum breezed through the door, flowers in one hand, a bag of fruit in the other. She kissed her daughter on the forehead. "How are you doing, my beautiful girl? You look better today."

"Thanks, Mum, I feel better."

"I brought you something nice to snack on and a collection of my organic beauty products. I thought you might like a makeover, like we used to do when you lived at home."

"Sounds great, Mum."

Lucy's mum laid out several mason jars filled with mud and oil.

"They smell amazing, Mum."

Izzy put a scarf around Lucy's hair to hold it back from her face. "You are such a pretty girl, dear Lucy."

"Mum, you always say that."

"Because it is true. Okay, head back, let's start with a cleanse." Izzy rubbed the coconut oil cleanser with a drop of lemongrass all over Lucy's face.

Lucy let out a sigh of relief as her mum massaged around her temples and jaw line. "It has been such a long time since we did this."

"Life gets busy. It is okay, Lucy, we can do better from now on."

"I would like that, Mum."

"Tell me to mind my business, but is everything okay between you and Tom?"

"Yes, I think so. He treats me well, understands my illness, helps with the kids. I worry he will get sick of me and the things I do sometimes. I thought maybe he was having an affair, but I do not know."

"Do you love him?"

"Yes, Mum, I have never stopped loving him," said Lucy.

"Well, that is good. I know he loves you, Lucy, and with love, you can sort out all the problems of the world."

"Mum, my turn for you to tell me to mind my own business."

"Go on."

"I remember when I was little, Dad yelling at you all the time. I remember you crying a lot, in the bathroom, in your bedroom, while driving, and shopping. You tried to hide it, but it didn't work. It seemed to go on for years. Dad and George weren't talking, and I always thought it was something that you both did to upset Dad, but then it stopped. No one ever told me why it started or why it ended. Did it end?"

"Lucy, why are you bringing all this up now?" Izzy wiped the cleansing oil from Lucy's face with firm stokes, contorting the shape of Lucy's face. "I do not like to think of those times, Lucy. I do not want to think badly of your father. He treated me poorly for a while. George, too, and I stopped loving him through all the anger and hurt. We tried family counselling, but he wouldn't cooperate, just kept listing all the things I did wrong, said it was my fault that George was the way he was. He was insecure, a child. I thought I was doing the right thing, giving him a lot of attention, but your father did not see it that way. All our arguments would always revolve back to George, no matter how they started. He was a troubled kid, but he needed more understanding than your father was prepared to give. Dad would just blow up. We made so many mistakes back then, and you, your poor sensitive soul, got caught up in the middle."

"Why did you stay?" asked Lucy.

"I stayed for you, and later, when your dad tried in his own clumsy way to make amends, we stopped fighting, mostly. George became independent, and I all but lost him. I lost my family because of those years. It broke my heart when your brother moved away. As much as I was pleased for him and Rupert to be going on an adventure together, I knew it was done. They never came back to Perth. Sure, I visit them, but there is no big family dinner for us, no happy family vacations, no big birthday bashes. Nothing, there never can be now your dad is gone." said Isabel.

"Did you love Dad in the end?" asked Lucy.

"Yes, I fell in love with him all over again. It took some trips to the counsellor to let go of the idea that I would ever have the family picture I so longed for. To compartmentalise my relationship with your dad, to my relationship with you and George, and most of the time, I was able. I can enjoy the moments. My family life is a tapestry, made of different relationships and many beautiful moments. Like this one." said Isabel.

"Do you think that is why George left?"

"I am sure it was part of it. It hurt him not to feel accepted. You and me loving him was not enough to make us a family. I think it has helped him to hold his own family closer. Look at his life, it revolves around them. It is wonderful to be a part of the whirlwind his family life is with three children, two dogs, and a menagerie of cats and other animals. It took a while, but George grew into a wonderful man. I am proud to call him my son."

Izzy smoothed the mask onto Lucy's face.

"Oh, Mum, that smells gorgeous. What is it?" asked Lucy.

"Kaolin, geranium, lavender, sandalwood, and a touch of carrot oil. It is divine."

"Seriously, I bet you are making a killing at the markets," said Lucy.

"I do all right, but I am doing better since you set me up on Etsy. I have a booming online business. Who would have thought? It is perfect for return customers and new ones. Just like you said it would be. I love that it gives me something to do, and I can do it anywhere I travel. Thanks Lucy." said Isabel.

"You are super welcome, Mum, but when are you going to let me help you write that book, on oils and treatments? You know so much it would be a shame not to share all your knowledge with the world."

"Now hush, you are just afraid I will die and take all my secrets with me one day, sweet Lucy. Now stop talking, your mask is setting. I am going to pop to the kiosk and get us a decent coffee. Close your eyes." She popped an eye mask over Lucy's eyes. "I will be right back."

Lucy heard the door close and noticed the music her mum had left playing. She breathed in the sweet, earthy smell that surrounded her and reminded her so much of home.

Izzy's voice startled Lucy. "I brought back some carrot cake too. The food in that kiosk is so much better than what I have seen being handed out here."

"Thanks, Mum," Lucy mumbled through her mask.

"Suppose we better get that off, so you have your cake and eat it too." She smiled.

Lucy rolled her eyes and climbed out of bed to the sink near the door to wash off the mask.

"Lukewarm water, Luce."

"Yes, I know, Mum."

When the last bit of mud was washed off, her skin tingled. A spritz from a blue bottle her mother pulled out of her bag, and she was fifteen at home having her mum help her deal with her acne.

"I am so lucky that you are my mother." She wrapped her arms around Izzy's neck and kissed her cheek.

"You both are. No one else in the world would put up with the shit that I have had to cope with. It wasn't all mother's day chocolates and flowers, you know." She winked.

"I know, Mum, and we do appreciate you—I know George does, and I definitely do." Said Lucy.

"Here." She handed her daughter a plate with a wad of carrot cake thick with cream cheese frosting and brimming with walnuts and raisins.

"It was hard on you when we were growing up. How did you stay calm?"

"Codeine, I am not going to lie. But thankfully that was a time when you could buy as much mersyndol as you needed. Without questions, it kept me calm. When things got too bad, I could double up a dose and sleep, cry myself to sleep, but sleep." said Isabel.

"That was the nights Dad was out," said Lucy.

"How do you know?" asked Isabel.

"We would hear you. George would take care of me when he was there, get me a glass of water, put the toilet light on for me if it was dark, let me watch television with him in his room."

"It was hard on him." said Isabel.

"It was. I remember him telling one time when you and Dad argued that it was all his fault and maybe he should go away. I begged him to stay. He said Dad hated him, but I told him that me and you loved him and that should be enough for him to stay."

"It wasn't a nice time for him, Lucy, Dad being so angry all the time; the poor kid felt like a stranger in his own home. There were nights when Dad was out, and we all sat around watching something on the television, then Dad would come home and just kind of grunt at us, I would try to distract him so George could finish watching the show with you, but it wouldn't work. You could cut the tension with a knife, and eventually George would go to bed, usually before the show was finished. The tension was so palpable. Each one blaming the other."

"I blamed Dad. He was the adult. It was up to him to act like a grownup," said Lucy.

"Yes, I thought the same, and because of that I tried to make it up to George. I struggled to keep hold of him after he moved out of our home. I nagged him every week to meet me somewhere for dinner. He went off the rails then. Sometimes I did not know how to help, and I had nowhere except the counsellor to turn. Your dad wasn't interested. Told me to talk to my friends. He did not want to know." said Isabel.

"That was harsh. He was the biggest part of the problem."

"Yes, he was."

"How could you forgive him?" asked Lucy.

"He eventually tried hard to make things right, but it was too late. George had gone too far, been hurt too much, and left to his own devices for too long. The rift never healed. Even up to the end, there was never peace between them." She wiped a tear from her eye.

"I am sorry, Mum." said Lucy.

"It's okay, it is a part of your story now, but what brought all this up?" asked Isabel.

"Today, the doctor had me go over my childhood and asked me what I remembered most. Dad and George came up, of course. To be honest, it is the only thing that I remember being wrong in my childhood."

"Do you think that their behaviour affected you any?" asked Isabel.

"No, though perhaps it made me less outgoing. I did not want attention knowing that my brother was left out in the cold, so to speak; it wasn't fair. I missed out on those family outings too, Mum. It's a shame we can't get that time back. When this is through, I am going to spend some time with George. I want to make sure that he knows I am his sister through and through; we are family. I want to get to know him, like I should have been able to when I was growing up." said Lucy.

"Can I come too?" asked Isabel.

Lucy laughed. "Of course, you can. I will talk to Tom and get it sorted. I will not be here for too long. I feel better already."

"You look it too, how is the cake?" Asked Isabel.

"Divine." Lucy said.

THE WEDDING

When her mum had gone, she was alone to rest and took to counting the tiles on the ceiling. Tile six was the day she married Tom. In her father's absence, George walked her down the aisle. Lucy and Tom married in a little church down south, only a small wedding with forty-three guests, but everything was meticulous. Each ruffle, each flower, each satin bow had its place. They wrote their own vows, a friend from uni wrote their wedding march, another gilded their invitations. It was perfection. It was just the way Lucy dreamt it would be.

She pulled out her phone from her bedside drawer, left herself a note to give her brother a call, arrange a trip, and spend time with her family. If only she was older before her dad had passed, knew more, done more. Maybe they could have had some family moments that Mum always longed for.

The newlyweds honeymooned in Bali, a cliche that they were both prepared to live with. Tom and Lucy slept late and luxuriated in massages, poolside lunches, and sunset walks along legion beach. Planning their future together. It was all going to be so easy: they would return to Fremantle, buy a house, have some kids, and love each other for the rest of their lives.

On the second last night of their honeymoon - they

were walking hand in hand along the tourist strip of Legian when a familiar voice yelled out from inside a bar,

"Hey, pigs arse we don't do them sort of extras!"

Tom and Lucy winced, turning to see Sam standing there with a bintang in one hand, wearing a barely there string coverall and a black bikini.

"Well, look at you two, I haven't seen you both since, well, that night you hooked up with my best waitressing partner." She wrapped her arms around both their necks and pressed herself to them. "Imagine seeing you two here!"

"Imagine," said Lucy.

"Your mum told me you got married. Lucky you!" said Sam.

"When did you see my mum?" asked Lucy.

"A week ago? Down at the markets, selling her wares."

"I am surprised to see you in Bali. You always said you hated *these kinds of places*, too third-world I think you said," Lucy said.

"Well, we are all entitled to change our opinion, don't you think? I have to say that I am disappointed in you. We have been friends for most of our lives and you get married without me," said Sam.

"It wasn't intentional. I sent you an invitation, and it came back return to sender. What was I supposed to do?" asked Lucy.

"I am on Facebook." said Sam.

"You weren't." said Lucy.

"Well, I was after I heard about your wedding. Your

photos are beautiful. I was just really sorry to have missed it. You looked amazing," said Sam.

"Thank you, Sam. We missed having you there too. I really tried to find you. Why don't we catch up for drinks sometime and you can tell me about everything you have been up to?" asked Lucy.

"How about now?" Sam asked.

"I was thinking about back in Perth, Sam. We were just heading back for an early night," said Lucy.

"Come on, a quick drink won't hurt. I promise not to hold you two love birds up for very long," said Sam.

Lucy and Tom looked at each other; it was an impossible situation they couldn't say no to.

"Of course," Tom said. "Let us buy you a drink at your hotel, save you walking home alone."

"No, let's go to yours. My hotel doesn't even have a bar, can you imagine?" said Sam.

"No, I can't," Lucy said.

"Alrighty, let's grab a cab," said Sam.

Tom ordered a round of drinks and visited the men's room, taking his time to give the two friends a chance to catch up. He didn't want to be in the middle of that conversation. There was no invitation, they both knew it. Maybe Sam did too. Sam was a part of the life Lucy was lucky to leave behind. And rightly so. He had already seen that Sam was a skeleton rattler. Maybe they would reconcile, and things would be okay, maybe they would grow apart and become distance memories in each other's pasts. He hoped the latter, returning to the table with drinks. The air was tight.

The next morning, Lucy noticed her throbbing head-first, then the feel of something wet and warm on her arm. She let the light slowly creep in through her eyes, groaned involuntarily at the throbbing in her ears. When the face on her arm came into focus, it shocked her to see that Sam's mouth was on her arm.

"Fuck! What the fuck are you going here? Where am I? Where is Tom?"

"Lucy, hello, baby. You woke up grumpy," said Sam.

"Don't you who fucking, "*woke up grumpy*" me. What are you doing here, in our hotel room, naked on our fuck-ing bed? What did you do?"

"Everything!" Sam smiled.

Lucy could barely focus as Sam watched her scan the room.

"Lover boy ended up calling for huey. He is probably still in the bathroom."

Lucy staggered to the bathroom to find Tom naked, sprawled out star fish on the porcelain tiles, bleeding from his head.

"Sam, call the doctor. Tom has been hurt."

"I am a doctor, he is okay. He did that last night, and he is still breathing."

"He did this last night. He was vomiting, and you thought it was okay to leave him here, alone? You did not think to call a doctor, did not think that he might need emergency care? What the fuck is wrong with you?"

"You did not think he needed emergency care, Lucy. You wanted us to keep fucking!"

"I did no such thing. I couldn't," said Lucy.

"Oh my god, you don't remember, do you?"

Lucy rolled a towel into a pillow and put it under Tom's head, used the bathmat to cover his nakedness and gently patted his cheeks. "Tom, it's me, you need to wake up!"

"No, he doesn't, Lucy, you need to remember!"

"No, I do not. I need to know that my husband is okay!"

"Stop being such a baby and come back into the bedroom and talk to me," said Sam.

Lucy grabbed the robe from the back of the bathroom door.

"You do not have to cover up for me. I have had my tongue all over that body you are now trying to hide."

"Leave, Sam, now."

"Don't you want to know what happened last night? You want to. I know you, Lucy. It is killing you to be out of control."

"Really, Sam, what are you trying to prove."

"That you still love me."

"I do not love you, Sam. I do not even like you. I want you to leave. Now."

Sam walked towards her, ran a hand along her hair. "No, you don't, you want to know what happened, how we got here. Remember, we were drinking at the hotel bar last night, then you ordered shooters, you were kissing Tom, then you kissed me, tongue and all. You were hot; Tom was got hard watching. He liked the action, I could tell. He ordered us more drinks. We closed the bar, then we came up here. We took turns between riding Tom's cock and his face. He came disappointingly quickly, then went to the bathroom. You were still horny, so I went down on you. We sixty-nined until you screamed and came all over my face."

"What happened to Tom?" asked Lucy.

"I do not know. He went into the bathroom and crashed. Literally." Sam laughed.

"He wouldn't have engaged in a threesome with you or anyone. What did you do, Sam?"

"I guess you two learnt a lot about each other last night."

"You must have put something in our drinks."

"Really, is that what you have to believe? Can't you see that you still love me, that all men are the same? Pathetic and easy to seduce. Your marriage means nothing, not to him, not to me, and not even to you."

"What! Why are you here? Why are you doing this to me?"

"Doing what? Exposing your holes?" asked Sam.

"I do not believe Tom had any part of this. You must have hit him, drugged him or something. He would have no part of you. He is better than that, better than you."

"Really, is that what you believe? Then taste his cock. The last pussy he was in was mine."

"I do not believe you."

"He wanted me badly. You wanted me badly."

"I do not believe you; you are a liar, Sam, always have been, always will be. I do not care why you are here, I just want you gone. Stay out of my life. Stay away from us, or I will—"

"What, little Lucy? What are you going to do? You make me laugh. Last night, you were ready to run back to

Perth with me. You wanted to live with me again like we used to when we were at uni before the man. Now you are being cruel to me, Lucy. You told lies you now pretend that I mean nothing to you. That we meant nothing?"

"Oh my god, is that what this is all about? Are you jealous? Afraid? What? Does it bother you that I moved on without you telling me what to do, ordering me around, treating me like shit and dumping me when it suits you! Leaving me without a word, deserted and alone. You!"

"Is that why you married that man? To get your revenge on me? That was a far stretch of revenge, Lucy. When are you going to tell him to fuck off and leave us alone?"

"Leave us alone? Sam, leave us alone. What the fuck do you think is going to happen now?"

"Isn't it obvious, Lucy, he cheated on you on your honeymoon? Doesn't that tell you something? He will cheat on you again. It is time to cut your losses and get the hell out. He doesn't deserve you, he is a liar and a cheater!"

"No! He is not. You tricked us both. This is your fault. I will not let you control me anymore, Sam, fucking get dressed and get out now! I will call security and get you thrown out!"

Left alone, she checked on Tom, still lying on the bathroom floor. "Tom." She shook him gently. "Tom, wake up, please." She shook him harder now. "Tom, wake up."

He groaned and reached a hand to his head. "What the hell."

"I think you fell. I woke up, you weren't in bed." He sat up and she helped him to his feet.

"Are you okay?"

"I think so, just a rotten headache, and a bruise," said Tom.

"A gash, actually, must have been from when you fell," said Lucy.

"Fuck, how much did we drink last night?" asked Tom.

"A lot. I remember shooters and not too much more after that," she offered.

"No, me either. One minute I was at the bar getting you and what's-her-name, another drink, I went to the toilet, and nothing. My mouth tastes disgusting. Did I throw up last night?"

"I do not know, I must have crashed when we got back here," said Lucy.

"Well, not right away, judging by the bed," he offered as he collapsed onto crumpled sheets.

Lucy lay down next to him. "I wonder what happened to Sam?"

"She must have left us at the bar. Sick of our antics, I suppose. It was weird her showing up out of the blue. Why didn't you invite her to the wedding?" asked Tom.

"I just want to leave her behind. I want to be with you, enjoy you and starting our life together. She was part of my single, pre-Tom life, and my life now is about you and me." said Lucy.

"You two have an interesting past, and I do not mind if you want to stay friends with her. Personally, though she makes me feel uncomfortable, there is something in the way she stares at me and you, for that matter, like she is trying to come on to me and you," said Tom.

"Yes, she can be intense."

"I love you, Lucy. I will not tell you who your friends should be."

"Thanks, babe." She passed him two Panadol and swallowed a set herself, closed her eyes, prayed that he had forgotten what went on last night. If anything went on, Lucy could not remember, and she knew what a liar Sam was. Closing her eyes, she felt secure in Tom's arms. All was right in her world for now, and she would not let Sam's games ruin her life again.

NEW KID IN TOWN

Lucy woke from her afternoon nap as the nurse came in to check on her.

"Tea will be around shortly," she chirped.

Lucy smiled and counted her way through to the eighth ceiling tile. *When did I first see Sam?* Sam was new to school. It was grade three. She was in Miss Botham's class. The scrawny little Asian girl wearing long wool socks and a grey pinafore. When Miss Botham introduced Sam to the class, she asked for a volunteer to be her friend and show her around the school. Lucy threw up her hand, keen to make friends with the interesting-looking creature, staring furiously around the class with her nearly black eyes.

It took most of the day, but Lucy made her new friend smile when she accidentally slipped and fell down the stairs leading from the portable classroom to the playground at the end of the school day. Sam laughed, said goodbye, and ran across the oval to jump the school fence with remarkable speed and agility.

Lucy stood there rubbing the bruise on her buttocks that the fall left. The pain was worthy of a tear, but she had been too curious to shed one. In the days that followed, the two girls sat together during class and ate lunch together, sharing cake and fruit while their awkward friendship grew. Lucy had been a loner at school before Sam came along. She read her books and weaved imaginary conversations in her head and often volunteered to help the teachers, any teacher, during the breaks. Sam was her first real friend.

Lucy asked her mum if she could invite Sam for dinner. Isabel had been overjoyed that Lucy had found a friend at school. She, of course, said yes, but it would be years before Sam ever walked through their door. It took Lucy's mum to issue an invitation in person to Sam's grandparents before she was allowed to visit. Then it was only for an hour, and her grandparents spent most of the time out on the footpath, waiting to pick her up. As this went on, Izzy would pop out to invite them inside for a drink, tea, anything. One particularly hot day she did not ask and went outside with two cold drinks to the footpath, begged them to come inside and see what the girls were doing. They refused politely but sternly.

They were both nine years old when the old man collapsed outside on the footpath while waiting for the girls to finish their homework. It really wasn't homework. They just played school with Sam as the teacher, finding weird and unusual ways of punishing Lucy for some imagined discretion.

Grandmother did not know what to do. She knocked rapidly upon the front door, and Izzy answered to an incomprehensible stream of broken English and Chinese. It was only when the old woman pointed to her husband with both hands that Izzy and the girls, drawn out by the ruckus, understood.

"Lucy, call an ambulance," Izzy said as she raced to the path.

While her mum was checking his vital signs, the grandmother clutched her hair, face and chest, speaking only in Chinese through her tears.

"Does he have a heart problem?" Izzy asked, visually acting out the words.

Inside, Lucy picked up the phone. Sam had grabbed it from her hand. "Here, let me call."

Lucy stood back and watched Sam dial 911.

"That is not the right number, Sam. You need to dial 000."

"No, I do not. You know nothing, Lucy Bell, it is 911."

"Here." Lucy tried to grab the phone from her friend, but Sam pushed her to the ground.

"I will call. I want to; he is my grandfather and I will call."

A voice on the other side of the phone answered, "You have reached emergency services; please be aware that your call was directed to 000."

"See," Lucy said, hearing the voice from the earpiece.

Sam hung up the phone. "It doesn't matter. Grandfather should die anyway."

"Sam! You can't do that! Call them back," said Lucy.

Lucy grabbed the receiver from Sam, who again pushed her hard with both hands and shunted her into the wall.

"Sam, my mum said that I have to call, so I am going to call. Your grandfather needs help or he will die."

"He should die. He is so old and stupid."

"Sam!" It was Izzy at the entrance to the kitchen. "Fetch your grandmother this water; Lucy, dial 000."

Izzy took a deep breath. "Kids!" Lucy passed her the phone.

The ambulance came, and the paramedics confirmed that Sam's grandfather had suffered a heart attack. Her grandmother accompanied him to the hospital, agreeing that Sam could stay at Lucy's. The girls were ecstatic and, wanting to lift the tension, Izzy suggested they head out to a movie and grab some food.

The outing served its purpose. When they pulled into the driveway of Lucy's home, Sam's grandmother was waiting on the front porch. She thanked Izzy for her help and told Sam that it was time to go.

"NO!" Sam had shouted. "I do not want to go home with you."

"Sam, it is time to come home. You do not live here."

"NO! I want to stay. You said I could stay. Why aren't you at the hospital with Grandfather?"

"Your grandfather is dead. He died at the hospital. We leave now."

Sam took the hand that the old woman held out. Grandmother thanked Izzy for her offered condolences, and she left with her granddaughter.

For the rest of that summer, Lucy would walk home from school alone. She would call by Sam's house on her walk home from school, but there was no answer to her knocking. They just disappeared.

Sam returned to school the following year. A young

lady in red heels brought her to class—Sam's mum had returned to raise her daughter and care for her mother.

A NEW DOCTOR

Sitting on the green chair across from the doctor, Lucy heard him ask, "You were diagnosed you with post-natal depression after the birth of your children?"

"Yes," said Lucy.

"Okay, let's talk about the pregnancy."

"Sure, how far back do you want to go?"

"Why don't we talk about when you first decided that you wanted a baby?"

"Well, we talked about it for ages, a couple of years. We had been married maybe four, five years, we were settled into our house and each other. It was a great time. Friends of ours had just found out that they were expecting, and we thought it was wonderful, and I guess we both just were ready. We decided together to stop trying not to get pregnant and see what happened. Three weeks later, I was pregnant."

"How was your pregnancy?"

"Hard. I had constant morning sickness, some weird, itchy skin rash no one could diagnose. I had headaches, backaches, joint pain, everything. Our business was insane. We had a couple of bleeds that scared the crap out of us, and two weeks before they were actually born, labour started. I dilated to 1 cm and then stopped. Nothing, so we brought them into this world through a caesarean."

"Did that disappoint you?"

Lucy frowned at the doctor across the desk.

"That you did not deliver naturally?"

"No, it did not bother me. They were healthy and beautiful. That is all that mattered."

"Yes, of course it is. It is just that some women find it upsetting if something alters their birthing plan, and that alone can trigger post-natal depression."

"I did not have a plan. I was just trying to survive the pregnancy. All I wanted was for healthy babies. I did not care what I had to do, feel, or go through to get them here."

"Of course, that is the wiser option. You cannot control childbirth, no matter how hard science tries. How was your recovery? Any complications?"

"I do not think so. To be honest, I cannot remember, I just remember being consumed by these tiny, beautiful little babies. All my attention went to looking after them and work and Tom."

"Did you take a break from work?"

"No, I couldn't, but what I did was mostly from home. The babies were always with me."

"Did the babies affect your relationship with your husband?"

"Yes, they slept in our room at first, then when it was time to move them into their own room, we had a single bed in there that I would sometimes sleep in, you know, if they were hard to settle. I did not want them waking Tom up through the monitor when he had to be up for work the next day. He would often wake me up in the middle of the night and tell me I was being stupid, that I needed to be in bed. He pretended he was worried I was not getting enough rest, but I felt like it was more that he felt I was neglecting him, that he was misplaced somehow."

"Interesting. When did you feel that something wasn't right?"

"I didn't. I was doing my job, taking care of my new-borns, looking after the business paperwork and delivery runs and the home as best I could while taking care of babies. I was tired, and yes, sure, I had little left at the end of the day. But I thought that was normal. Tom didn't think so. He kept saying he was worried, that I seemed sad, that he thought that there was something wrong. He kept saying that I was changing."

"Were you changing?"

"Yes, I was a mother, so yes, I changed, but that was all. I was a mother."

"Was Tom active in taking care of the babies?"

"When he was home, but he was hardly home."

"How did that make you feel?"

"It was not what I wanted, but it was what I was used to. My dad worked long hours too, and I do not remember him ever being around much or even being there when he was home. So, it was what I was used to. I guess I hoped that somehow my life would be different, but Mum managed, so I guess always thought that I would too."

"When did it all get too much for you?"

"We argued one night, I was sleeping in the babies' room. They both had a cold, and it worried me, first time mum and all, so I slept on the spare bed with the cot drawn right up next to me. The next morning, I was tired, and he was snapping at me. It annoyed me he thought his needs were more important than the babies. I told him he was an adult and sometimes he would have to learn to look after himself."

"How did he take it?"

"He did not speak properly to me for days. I would make dinner and he would tell me he wasn't hungry, or text me from work saying he was going straight to the gym, and he would find himself something to eat. He would hang his work clothes up rather than put them in the laundry. I let him, and he wore the same shirt to work for four days. His sulk exploded into an argument and he stormed out, left me in tears. When he finally came back, it wasn't to apologise. He just twisted things to make it my fault that there was something wrong with me. I was obsessing over the babies and perhaps I needed to see someone. I thought he could be right. We had never argued like that before, and maybe I wasn't taking care of him properly. It wouldn't hurt to find out, and if it turned out that I was okay, maybe he would have to change."

"Sounds like you only agreed to see someone to prove your husband wrong."

"Yes, I did. I really did not believe that there was anything wrong with me. I have always suffered premenstrual syndrome and got the sads a few days a month. This wasn't that I was just feeling tired. At least, that is what I thought."

"How did Sam become your doctor?"

"My GP referred me to Sam. She was highly recommended for post-natal and women's health, plus she was bulk billed, so I wouldn't be adding an unnecessary drain to our budget. She knew me. I was sure at the time that would be a good thing." Lucy took a drink of water and paused.

"Go on, please."

"Well, Sam was all professional from the outset. She told me that although we had a history, she believed she could put that aside and help me through whatever I was going through. I trusted her. She seemed genuine, so I spent the next two hours filling out online questionnaires to test my mood. Then she told me to go home, with some tablets to take every night and morning with food and booked me in the following week."

"What happened that week?"

"It was awful. I couldn't sleep. I felt nauseous all the time. I was forgetful, and slow, just slow. Tom started looking after the babies more. I think he was genuinely worried. I do not think it occurred to him that my symptoms got worse only after seeing Sam."

"What happened when you went back to see Dr Huong?"

"Sam was nice, made me a cup of tea, gave me a biscuit, sat me down on the couch. Acted really concerned. She said, Lucy, I do not know how to tell you this, but your results are not good. You are suffering from a severe level nine post-natal depression. I am afraid without help you and your babies are in danger."

"How did you respond?"

"I asked her how, what was she talking about it. She told me it was common for mothers with post-natal depression to separate themselves from their husbands, move into the baby's room, insisting that they are only doing what is best for the baby, and then they later become so pissed off that the baby they try so hard to serve is taking so much from them they try to harm the baby, sometimes by making them ill, frequent colds or tummy bugs. I denied it. To which she told me that of course I wasn't doing it consciously, that I had an imbalance that was causing me to act strange, to not feel myself, that I was dangerous."

"Did Dr Huong carry out any blood tests before this diagnosis?"

"No, she never sent me for any. Should she have?"

"That she didn't is a definite red flag. Please go on, Lucy, you are doing really well."

"She prescribed some more medication. Tom brought it all, and my mum gave it to the nurse when I checked in. She misdiagnosed me, didn't she?"

"Yes, I believe she did. I think that what you had originally been a case of pissed-off wife syndrome, you were tired, you were recovering from major surgery, you felt isolated and let down by a husband that criticised you for giving every ounce of energy you had to looking after twin babies. Sometimes partners like to think that something other than our own selfishness is wrong when our partner is distracted by taking care of the children."

"All of this is not Tom's fault. I can't let him take all the responsibility or put the blame on him. He was as misguided as I was."

"Yes, of course. It is not Tom's fault. The only person to blame here is Sam. She deceived you, mistreated you, misdiagnosed you, and frankly broke the law by treating you for a condition that you clearly did not have. You have been poorly treated, and I will submit my report to the Australian Medical Association this afternoon with a recommendation that Dr Halong has her license suspended awaiting a hearing."

"Do you think she has done this to other women?"

"Maybe, however, maybe she was seeking revenge specifically on you after the opportunity arose to treat you. What we need to work on now is getting you past this and accepting that the person you thought you were is not who you are. That you were perfect at the birth of your children and you would have stayed that way without Dr Huong's interference. Get some rest. We will talk again tomorrow."

ONE HOT SUMMER

In the middle of the hot West Australian summer, Lucy ran home early from school. It was school policy back then, when kids all walked to and from school, to let them go home early. Nothing much got done on a scorching afternoon when most of the classrooms did not have an air conditioner.

They locked the house up, so she climbed up the side fence into the backyard and squeezed through the doggy door at the rear of the house. Hudson, the German shepherd, heard her and licked her face as she wiggled her butt through. The house was quiet except for the radio that was always on in the upstairs bathroom. She poured herself a glass of orange juice, grabbed a bag of potato chips, then headed up to her room.

On her way, she heard noises from her parent's bedroom, muffled church sounds of "*oh god*" and "*Jesus.*" Lucy approached the door to look through the crack and could see her dad on top of the man that cleaned the pool. His legs were wide in the air, like a woman Lucy had seen on the television late at night, but his arse was flat and covered in hair, and there was a cock and balls where his yoni should be.

They could didn't see her from behind the door, even with Hudson wagging his tail and licking her hand in need of a treat. Lucy crept quietly down the hall to her own room and secured herself inside with Hudson lying at the door standing watch. When the sounds of the bed stopped, she heard regular man-sized voices, then there were footsteps around the room and up and down the hall away from her room. Lucy did not move. She did her best to hold her breath for as long as she could, taking only little sparrow breaths so as not to make a sound. She could not to let on that she was here, interrupting something that she should not have seen. Even when she heard her father's car drive out of the garage and down the road, she could only move in baby steps onto her own bed, where she laid face down with her hands over her ears and her eyes squeezed tightly shut.

Lucy kept what she had seen to herself until the eve of her sixteenth birthday. Her dad had returned home from work in a foul mood, stomping around yelling at her mother about something to do with work. It eventuated that she had added the wrong contract number to an invoice, and the company had rejected it. Lucy heard everything, and she had enough. She stormed down the stairs and told her dad to shut up and leave her mother alone.

He was being a bully, she continued, and Mum deserved better.

"Lucy," her mother scolded, "you stay out of this. It is none of your business."

"Yes, it is. I live in this house too, and what happens

here is as much my business as it is yours. What happens here affects me too."

"Yes, it does," her father answered, "but what happens here is my business, not yours. You get to live here by the grace of all that is my business, so you will treat me with the respect I deserve."

"I already do!" Lucy yelled.

"Is that right? Well, you can forget about your fancy party tomorrow night that has your mother all distracted. Ring your friends and tell them it is off."

She stared at her father, defiantly holding back tears. "I will tell them why, that my bully of a father is nothing but a faggot pig!"

"Lucy!" her mother exclaimed as Lucy turned and run up the stairs back to her room.

"I will talk to her," said Isabel.

"What did she call me?"

"I said I will talk to her."

"I am not backing down."

"Yes, I know you are not, and a fine way she has now to remember her sweet sixteen."

"It is not my fault! You fucked up!"

"Yes, I know," she said to his back as he exited the kitchen door out into the carport. She waited until she heard his car going up the street and away. She did not care where but assumed it would involve drinking. Knocking on the door of her daughter's room, Izzy could hear her muffled crying into a pillow.

"Lucy, it's Mum. Can I come in?"

"Yes."

As her mother opened the door, Lucy said, "I am sorry, Mum, I had to say something. He cannot keep treating you that way."

"Lucy, sometimes you have to understand that your dad gets stressed, and, well, he doesn't quite know how to handle it."

"Mum, why the fuck are you making excuses for him? He drove George away. He treats you like shit, and I know he has been fucking the pool man!"

"Lucy, why are you saying these things? I am sorry that your father cancelled your party, but there is no need to say such cruel things. Your father has never been unfaithful to me, and he certainly is not fucking the pool man. We will sort something else out for your birthday. Tell your friends that the house has a flea infestation, and I will send you all to a bowling party. Time zone? The movies? Ice skating? Anywhere you want to go, Lucy. Let me make it up to you."

"You, you make it up to me? You have done nothing wrong, except for now, you are not hearing what I am telling you. You are not listening to me."

"Lucy, I know you mean well, but that is between me and your father. That argument was between me and your father, and one day when you grow up you will realise that marriage is hard. It is not all soap operas and fairy tales, it is tough. Tough to live with someone day in and day out, to constantly compromise the things that you want to do, especially when you find out that you not only married a man you married a lifetime career of taking care of his shit at work and at home. It is a full-time job that I did not sign up for."

"Mum stop lying to me. He is a hypocrite. Dad is gay!"

"Your father is not gay Lucy, he is bisexual, or whatever they call it now."

"You know?"

"Of course, I know, and I am curious to know how you know."

"Back in grade seven, I came home early from school. It was summer, thirty nine degrees, and they let us come home early. No one was home, or so I thought. I climbed the fence and squeezed through the dog door, grabbed some snack, and headed up to my room to get an early jump on my homework when I saw dad getting an early jump on our pool man, Mr Horatio. It doesn't make any sense that dad is gay, he is always so angry, nothing kind about him or creative. How can you stay with him? Knowing what you know and putting up with the way he treats you."

"Because you need a home, you need two parents. I need your father because—and you won't understand this —but we do love each other, Lucy. He really is bisexual, not gay. He loves me. We are sexually active, but sometimes he craves the attention of a man. I understand that because I do too. How can I deny your father something when I want the same?"

"Because he is cheating on you."

"No, he is not. We agreed early in our marriage that he would discreetly follow his cravings. He has been with

Mr Horatio for many years now, and on the upside, we get our pool cleaned for free."

"Is Mr Horatio gay or bi?"

"He is bisexual too. I know, what are the odds?"

"If dad is not so angry because he is a repressed homosexual, then what the fuck is the matter with him, Mum, why is he so childish and unreasonable?"

"Stress. At least, that is what I put it down to. A lifetime of stress."

"Then why the fuck doesn't he go and speak to a shrink?"

"He should, but he won't. We have had our share of arguments over that topic, and quite frankly I am done. I see a counsellor, and I feel better for it. I tried to get your father to come along and he will not have a bar of it, but my counsellor told me that sometimes it is good enough for one person to change, sometimes this lets the other person come along too. Not always, but over the years it has been easier. Dad will come home. Apologise at some point,

and we will again be fine for a while."

"But you don't deserve it, Mum, not how he treats you."

"What do I deserve, Lucy? Life is not so much about getting what you deserve, it is about only taking on the load you can carry. Please let it go, Lucy. Let us focus on you and what you are going to do about your birthday party tomorrow."

"Do I really have to cancel, Mum?"

"No, it is not cancelling, it is just changing the venue. What about a suite at the Esplanade?"

"No way. Are you serious?"

"Yes, why not? I will get a room near you to act as a chaperone. We will pick your friends up as usual to-morrow and surprise them."

"You are the best, Mum." Lucy wrapped her arms around her neck and planted a kiss on her cheek.

TOM

Tom fumbled around the in the dark for his phone. "I understand, and I will be right there," he answered, the voice on the other side.

It was too early to ring Izzy. It would take him four hours to get there anyway, and chances were there would be nothing he could do. Driving through sunrise, he reached the hospital at seven thirty, parked in an emergency bay, and ran up the front steps through the double doors and on to Lucy's room. Bursting through the door, he found her sleeping.

"Excuse me," he said to the nurse passing, "is everything okay with my wife, Lucy Ballard? I received a call yesterday. Well, last night, saying that she had fallen and hurt her head. That she needed stitches across her forehead? But look, she is fine."

"I am sorry, Mr Ballard, but I was the only nurse on all night here, and your wife is fine. I do not know who called you, but it was not me. Lucy is fine. I believe there is a plan for her to be released in the next day or two to outpatient care."

He stared blankly. "Why? Oh, fuck." He turned to run out the way he came back into the carpark. It was deserted. "What have I done?"

Pulling his phone from his pocket, he called Izzy and brought her up to speed.

"It appears you have been tricked, but don't blame yourself. I would have done exactly the same thing," she offered.

"What do we do now?" asked Tom.

"I suggest we get Lucy out of there as soon as possible and that you contact that police sergeant so that he can let the local coppers know what is going on. And keep your eye out, Sam could be anywhere."

"I have to get back to Perth for a work meeting—we need the work, we need the money," said Tom.

"Go on, I can handle things here," said Isabel.

"I am going to wait with Lucy until you get here and let her know what is going on," said Tom.

"Good, I will grab a quick shower and I will be down there soon. Can I bring you anything?"

"Coffee, would be nice," said Tom.

"Of course." said Isabel.

"Thank you, and again, I am sorry."

"Stop saying that you are sorry. This is nobody's fault, no one's fault except Sam's, anyway."

He kept watching in his rear-view mirror, hoping that Sam was behind him, that he could catch her out. He made it back to their Fremantle home in time to shower and to head out for his meeting, feeling secure that Lucy was safe with her mum and no one but them, the police, and he knew where they were.

The detectives found Sam's home empty. She had moved on and left the place immaculate. The agent told them she had to leave quickly for a family emergency and paid up the lease in its entirety with no expectations of returning, no forwarding address. Immigration showed no signs that she had left the country at all, and as far as they knew, she had no family remaining, since her mother's suicide in 2012.

Lucy's mother joined her on the window seat and passed her a cup of tea and said, "Look, we have a police guard; that Sam has got us all into some scary shit now!"

"I'm sorry, Mum," said Lucy.

"Now then, there is no need for you to apologise. It is not your fault that she is a stark-raving mad bunny boiler!"

"You always warned me that something wasn't right with her."

"To be honest, I just thought that she was sad and jealous and more than a little mean, the way she would come and tell me things about you as if to shock me, get you into trouble, or worse change the way I would see you. She never understood a mother's love, probably because of the way her own mother was. She never knew that a mother's love is unconditional. Sure, you see your children make mistakes and they do things you wish they wouldn't for their own sakes, but you never stop loving them and you never stop being there for them. That is not how motherhood works. Instead of being shocked, I always made out that I knew already, shrugged my shoulders like it was no big deal; I wouldn't give her the satisfaction of feeling like she had one up on you. That is not how friends should behave. I understood that her family were different, so maybe she didn't realise how they worked or rather how they should work, rather how this one worked when I had my way. But that aside, you were a good friend to her, always. She should have learnt through you what a good friend was and mirrored the gifts you gave her. The support, the love, the discretion."

Tom pulled himself out of the car and slumped up the stairs to his front door, grateful to be home. He had just spoken to Lucy, and she sounded great, happy to be with her mum, happy with the outcome from the psychiatrist's examinations. All these years wasted. He was pissed. What sort of person would do that? He shuddered. He had let her seduce him. The memory of her made bile rise to the back of his throat, prickly heat to his face. The inevitability of Lucy finding out now took the strength from his legs as he stumbled through the front door. Would she, could she, ever forgive him? It was his fault that she went to the doctors in the first place because he was being a selfish, sooky prick upset because she wanted to look after their kids more than she wanted to fuck him! He felt like an asshole.

Tom needed to speak to her. He picked up his phone, dialled the number, and stopped himself. He knew he could lose everything, yet still believed that it had to come from him. Not some random police officer, her mother, or worse, from Sam herself. It should be him. He thought of her and saw her face before him. He saw her heart breaking, the pain on her face and the tears that only he has caused.

The phone slipped to the floor, and he moved to the

kitchen and poured himself a heavy shot of whiskey and slammed it down. It burned his throat and raised his bile, but he still poured another just as thick and slammed it down. Tom took the bottle and left the glass behind in the bathroom. He undressed and left the water running a little too hot. Still undressing he stepped under the water and cried while the pain in his chest took over him. He was a selfish prick. This was all his fault; if he had thought more about Lucy, then Sam could never have touched them. He was so blinded and childish. He remembered that night on their honeymoon that Sam crashed. She was hot—not that Lucy wasn't, but together they were every man's dream. He wanted that again, not his worn-out, tired mother-wife. That wasn't supposed to happen when you had a baby. No one told him that the father didn't matter anymore, that he did not have to have his needs met. It was all about the baby and the tired wife. Fuck, he was a selfish bastard.

The drink was going to his head faster than normal. The bathroom got a slow spin on it, and he staggered to make his way from the ensuite to the bedroom. He fell flat on the mattress, arms and legs star fished, naked and wet on the sheets.

"Finished, my little cry baby?" came a voice from above him.

He heaved himself around on his back. Tom couldn't sit up; he had lost control of his arms and legs. "Get the fuck out of my house, you mad bitch!" He slurred.

"Shhh, do not say things you do not mean, Tom. I know you love me and want me more than any other woman on the planet. So do not say things you will later regret."

"I do not want you, I want my Lucy."

THE TRAP

She slapped him hard across the face. Then his robe was being wrapped around him. There is someone else there. But he can't focus now. His arms and legs were lead weighted, and he couldn't move them. They were too heavy; he was weak.

The chilled night air hit his skin before they rolled him into the back of a van. He smelled paint, he tried to see, but now there was a bag on his head, he smelled paint, and then he was gone.

He woke to the smell of frangipanis, the sound of his blood thumping in his ears. His arms and legs were tied to all four corners of the bed, a satin sheet covering him. He could make out his robe over the back of the chair in the room's corner. *Fuck,* he thought, trying to get himself loose. *The bitch has dragged me back to her place.... How the hell did she manage it?* Why the fuck did he care? He had to get out of here.

"Ahh, my sleeping beauty, I see you are finally awake!" She swooped into the room dressed only in a red, silk, kimono, untied enough to show that she was naked underneath, a way of hers he once admired, how she could reveal everything while making you want to see more. Trouble was, now he had seen everything.

"What are we doing here, Sam? Why do you have me

tied here? I told you I want nothing more to do with your games."

"My games? This is not a game, Tom. You are here at my house while Lucy is in Albany with her mum. Only you and the police know where that is." She laughed.

"You do not know where Lucy is. You are lying. She is nowhere near Albany."

"Liar." She slapped his face hard. "No more lies, Tom. I just want us to spend one last night together and we can leave our separate ways, go about our own lives, and I will disappear forever. You owe me that much."

She climbed on top of him. There was a camera hanging from the light above her bed filming them; he could see the light was on as she unleashed a line of kisses down his torso.

He mouthed, *Lucy, I love you, I can't move, I do not know how I got here. Lucy, I love you.*

Sam took his cock into her mouth. After several moments of sucking and licking, it continued to lie like a large meat slug in her mouth.

She slaps it away. "What the fuck is a matter with you, brewers drip lover? I cannot fuck you with that."

"I do not want to fuck you, Sam. I told you that. I can't help it if I do not find your psycho bitch ways exciting. You can't make me want you, Sam, so just let me go. Please."

"No, I do not think so, you dumb fuck. I am a doctor, remember, and I can get any fucking thing I want."

"You are not a doctor anymore. They have struck you off for malpractice. They know what you did to Lucy, how you drugged her, how you made her think she was nuts, when all the time you were just manipulating her and me to do what you wanted. The gig is up, Sam, your office and records have already been raided, your records are being scoured for more cases of malpractice, and the police are looking for you and they will find you and carry your fat arse off to jail." said Tom.

"I do not have a fat arse!"

"Really, that is what you are taking from everything that I have just told you!"

"You take it back, lover, I do not have a fat arse!"

"You do. That is why my dick refuses to go hard for you."

She left him alone, and he pulled hard on his restraints. He couldn't loosen them or even make the bed move. He was alone for hours before she came back with a glass of water and a pill.

"Here, lover." She pushed it down his throat and took her fingers away before he thought to bite her. More water was offered; he was thirsty, and he drank. Inevitably, she will have her way. Until he worked his way loose, he would have to play along enough to let her drop her guard. She obviously wanted to be in control, so he was going to let her think she was.

She left him alone again. He stared at the ceiling, knowing he was being watched through the camera. It took some time, but it eventually became apparent that she had given him a Viagra pill to swallow. Without assistance, his cock tented the satin sheet. He tried to think of the things that made his cock soft: grandmothers, Sam being a psycho as opposed to Sam being a sex fiend. Lucy being hurt made his cock bend slightly, but then Sam appeared at the door in red suspender stockings and heels with nothing else. She strode in and straddled his cock in a single movement.

He closed his eyes tight and looked away. "No, Sam," he said, "Please get off me. I do not want to do this."

"Keep begging me, lover, keep lying to me. You know you want this, you love my pussy."

She was off his cock and rubbing herself on his face. "Lick me, lover."

Tom couldn't; he was smothered in her, her come over his face; he turned his mouth to the side so that her cunt was rubbing over his ear and he was yelling into her thigh.

"Get off me, Sam."

She left his face and straddled his cock with her back towards him. Ignoring his protests, she rode him until he came.

Sam lifted herself from him and, with her face an inch from her his, hissed, "You are mine. I will take what I want from you. I control you and your magnificent cock, and we can do this the hard way or the easy way. The choice is yours, lover, but you will be mine. I will see that Lucy never makes it back from Albany with that meddlesome mother of hers. Do things my way and your children will still have frigid mummy, and you can have me."

She left him alone, the smell of her all over his face. He couldn't wipe himself clean. He awoke several hours later to the sounds of Sam in his room.

"What do you want from me, Sam?"

"I told you things to go back to how they were, when

you and Lucy would let me control things. I don't want a husband. Husbands are bad people who take advantage of women, force them to have sex with them, yell at them when they do not keep the house clean or when dinner is not ready, or if they get fat, if they get sick, or if for one minute their husbands think they do not want to have relations with them. I do not want that. I want a regular cock though, without a man who wants to marry me or turn me into a mother. I do not want that. Which is why after our honeymoon in Bali, I orchestrated you and Lucy to be my fuck couple? Lucy is harder to get into bed than you ever were. I was in the middle of tweaking her medications so that she would still have no desire for you, because I couldn't have you fucking her too. I saw how you looked at her that night. I do not want to see that again. You don't even look me in the eye when we fuck, ever! Anyway, I was trying to get it so that Lucy would still fuck me too, like in the old days before there was you."

"The old days, when you and Lucy were an item, is that what this is about?"

"Yes, that was not that long ago, but when she met you, she said that she did not want to be with me anymore. You ruined it."

"I am not the reason that you two broke up. You were already gone. I remember Lucy told me how upset she was to think that you deserted her. She told me she woke up one morning after drinking too much wine alone waiting for you to come home and that she found you and all of your things gone. No word, nothing. Why did you do that to her?" asked Tom.

"Because she broke our rule."

"Which was?" he ventured.

"We both agreed that we would never bring our work home with us. Then she brought a fat, biker dude home for three hundred bucks to fuck her while I videoed it for him. When I refused, he beat me, broke two ribs and smashed my nose in. She left me there unconscious while she fucked him in our bed. I could not stay there. I was afraid. You believe me, don't you?"

He looked on at her, waiting to see where she went.

"You think that poor, innocent Miss Lucy would never do such a thing? Lucy would never be a prostitute. Does it hurt to think that she would not even give to you those things that she so cheaply sold to all of those other men? I wonder if it was that that made her hate sex so much. Sex with men, anyway. Well, more specifically, sex with you. Everyone is so quick to blame me. Yet what were you doing to make Lucy want you again, Tom? Did you look after her? Did you stay home from practise to help her take care of the babies, to sit and watch television with her, to bring her flowers, to spoil her spontaneously at any time? Tom, tell me, what did you do?" Sam asked.

"I did exactly what you told me to do. I went about my business, keeping myself happy so that she would not have to worry about me, so she would feel like I was doing okay, and sometimes to stop her from feeling useless, I would ask her to help me with work stuff. I did the things that you told me to do. Things that you said would make her feel better."

"Do not blame me, Tom. I am not your master. You

have a brain in the head of yours. You do not need me to tell you the right way to treat your wife. Let's not argue, love." She takes a cloth from the basin, the basin that she had brought in, and left on the side table. She squeezed the excess water out and brought it to him and gently washed his face, his chest, groin, and the length of his arm and legs in turn.

She left the room, and he was grateful that he couldn't smell her as much on his skin, but he felt desperate to go to the toilet, so much so that he was relieved to see her again.

"You must need to pee," she said girlishly.

"Yes, I do, but..." He opened his tied hands in a helpless, shrugging gesture.

"No worries," she said and pulled a hospital pee bottle from behind her back and pushed it over his exposed penis so that it sat inside.

"No, Sam, please let me go to the toilet properly."

"You can, here."

"I can't go with you watching me," he tried.

"Fine." She turned her back.

He couldn't hold it anymore. Ashamed to be completely at her mercy.

When he was done, she took the bottle to the ensuite, flushed the contents, rinsed the receptacle, and returned with it to the bedroom, popping it into a bedside drawer.

"Sam, if you really want this time we have here to be special, me peeing in a hospital cup is not the way to go about it. Untie me, let me hold you and make love to you properly. This is not the way."

"Do you think I am stupid, Tom? I know all you are thinking about is Lucy when we fuck. You do not look at me."

"Yes, I do. You are hot, Sam, you know you are. You turn me on, you make me forget I am married, when I am with you I forget my vows and promised to Lucy."

"No, you don't. I know how desperately your try to rub me off in the shower after you fuck me. There is no love for me in you. I want to show you that video and let's see how you feel for Lucy after you see how hot she is for other men. All it takes is money."

"No, Sam, I do not want to see it. That is not who Lucy is now."

"Really, Tom, how do you know? Remember where you met Lucy? The stag do before that one. She let six boys have her on the bar."

"I already know about Lucy, she told me, and about the boys. Well, why did you think our group specifically requested you and Lucy? We knew what happened. Sam, this is not the way to get me to love you. Destroying another person is no way to make someone love you more, it is not a competition. I am sorry that I mistreated you, took you for granted. If you feel that I never saw you but let me see you now, not the destroyer of other people's reputations but as Sam, my Sam."

"That will never work, Tom."

"Why not, Sam, we could be together," he tried.

"There you go again. You did not listen to a word I said, did you? You just think about how you want everything to be, assume I want the same, and focus on that. Well, I am not your bride!"

She stormed out of the room.

A PLAN

Sitting across from each other at opposite ends of the window seat, both women were half reading their books with their tea at their sides when Lucy's phone dinged.

Her mum watched her read the message.

"That is strange," said Lucy. "I just got a text message from Tom, saying that he is working late and can't talk. That I should get some rest because he has a surprise for me in the morning."

"That doesn't sound too strange," said Isabel.

"Except that it is longer than normal I usually get, "can't talk home late," said Lucy.

"Well, maybe he is trying to do better now?"

"Mum, I think Tom has been having an affair."

"Probably, dear. How do you feel about it?"

"That was a little too accepting, mother," said Lucy.

"Well, your babies are eight years old and you have been frigid since their birth. You would hardly expect him to not of had an affair, dear. Sorry, Lucy, I am sure that he feels like a right selfish shit for it now."

"Mum, do you know something?" said Lucy.

"No, I am sorry. I know nothing I intend to share other than this: if something happened, then it was done under exceptional circumstances that was no fault to either of you, and think seriously about forgiving the lad."

"Jesus, Mum, do you know who it was?"

"Sam. That manipulative bitch has been trying to break up your marriage and keep Tom to herself. It is her you can be angry at."

"Oh, and I suppose he just fell, and his dick slipped in? This is not Dad and the pool man."

"Well, it kind of is, Lucy. I slept with both of them too. Horatio was bisexual just like your father."

"Oh my fucking god, mother."

"You need not OMG me, young lady. Sam told me all about you two too."

"Not when I was married, Mum. I was always faithful to Tom, and now I find out that those two were fucking behind my back and you told me to forgive and forget?"

"Not quite, dear. You need an apology from him. He needs to promise that he will never do it again, that he will always love you like I know he always has. And then in time, you will forgive him. In time, you will stop wondering if he is seeing you when you are making love. Eventually you know he is, after years of insisting that he use your name in bed to reassure you. What else are you going to do, Lucy?"

"Leave him and come down here to live with you and start my life again without Sam and without Tom."

"Is that what you want, truly?"

"No, of course it is not. I want my marriage back the way it should have been before that bitch started fucking around with it. I want my husband to not have been a self-ish prick and helped me with the babies instead of saying that there was something wrong with me, and then Mum, and this is big, I want my husband to keep his cock in his pants long enough to realise that all he ever needed to do was to stop being such a selfish prick and blaming his marital problems on everything other than his own deep neglect of his wife."

"That's a girl. Get angry, fight for what you need. Fight for what you want and don't you dare let anyone take anything that you are not prepared to give. Do you understand, Lucy?"

"Yes. Mum. I am going to get my life back, and that means Tom too."

TOM

A light streamed into the room, hot on his face. His hands were numb from being strung to the bedposts. He was hungry, he could smell bacon cooking. Then she waltzed in like many times before, breakfast on a tray, with coffee, toast, and fruit.

"Ready for my special, anytime breakfast, lover?"

Although unwilling, he nodded and made a gesture to show that his arms were still tied.

"I would like to enjoy your fine breakfast, but, well, I would not enjoy being fed like a baby, so I will have to say thank you, but no thank you."

"Hmm, that is not good enough. Can I trust you, Tom? Trust you to give me just the next few days of us being together to give us a chance?"

"Yes, Sam, of course you can."

"You say yes, but I am not convinced."

"How can I hold you in my arms if I cannot wrap them around you?"

She took a knife from the tray, knelt across him, and sliced open one of the snatch straps securing him to the bed. "That is enough for now. You only need one hand to eat."

"Of course, Sam, that is very kind of you. Thank you. Sam, I was thinking, maybe we could go out today?" he said casually as he took a big drink of the coffee she tainted.

"No, Tom, I do not think so. I have some work to do today."

Tom ate some bacon; his head was feeling fuzzy; took a bite from the croissant and was gone.

"There's a good boy, Tom. I want you to behave yourself today. I need to pay your mummy a visit and check on the kids."

THE BREAK-IN

Under a weighted jacaranda tree outside 8 Matson St, Sam sat in her rental car, keeping a watchful eye on their house. She wanted to avoid involving the kids and was patiently waiting for their return from school drop off. So, she waited, and when it hit ten o'clock, she drove past the school looking for their car, then back to the house. When she got fed up with waiting, she walked up to the front door. She knocked, and when no one answered, she found her way around the back despite the protests of the family's Labrador.

She peered through the open blinds that looked out onto the pool and gazebo. Sure that no one was home, she took a small rock from the garden bed and smashed it through a window on the ten light laundry door, unlocked the lever, and let herself inside.

Down the hall and through to the kitchen, she creeps down the hall past Marty & Jonah's second bedrooms and steps into the master bedroom. An open suitcase was on the bed, a collection of old luggage tickets next to it.

"What's going on?" she said to no one.

The next room was the old man's den, a calendar on the wall with yesterday's date circled. 'Cruise'.

"Crap, they are not here."

The noise from the front door being opened caught her off guard.

"Henry," a voice came. It was the pet sitter. She had gone straight to the laundry to greet him at the door and attempted to stop him in his tracks when she saw the broken glass. But nothing would stop the lovable goof from getting to his beloved sitter.

"Oh, Henry, you silly goof, what have you done? It looks like you have had a visitor. And not a very nice one."

He didn't care and ran around her in circles, keen for his treat, a belly rub, and a walk.

Sam, upstairs listening, coughed involuntarily.

"Shh," said the sitter, "did you hear that? I think someone is upstairs." As she reached for her phone in her back pocket, Sam swiftly descended the stairs, snatched a cricket bat, and struck her from behind.

Henry barked and snarled at her until he got a treat and was ushered into the yard. Sam dragged the sitter up the stairs and into the guest room. Sam found tape in the kitchen and secured her, star fished, to the corners of the bed.

Sam went through the sitter's phone looking for a sign she would attract any attention if she went missing. Satisfied that the sitter had fewer friends than she did and Henry was the last dog for the day, she fed the pup, cleaned up the glass, took the spare key from the kitchen hook, and left.

TOM

Back in Sam's new apartment, Tom was stirring. He had a hand free and if he was smart, he felt sure that he would have another free tonight. "You just have to play it smooth," he said to no one. Despite himself, he needed to urinate and filled the hospital bottle she left him, covering it with a napkin from the tray she had left so he did not have to look at it. He picked at the food left on the tray, sipped the warm juice and cold coffee.

He slept, and when he woke up, he felt her lying at his side, his loose arm around her waist. With his eyes still closed, he thought he could fight her there, strangle her unconscious perhaps, but he knew he couldn't loosen the other cable tie. He was trapped, and she was his lifeline.

"Will you make love to me tonight, Tom?" she whispered in his ear.

He opened his eyes slowly, saw the blinking light of the camera. She was always recording when they were together. He couldn't play along and have Lucy think that he willingly slept with Sam. He whispered back into her ear,

"I like it when you force me."

"Do I have to give you that pill again?"

"Yes, I will not fuck you without it."

He watched her naked form leave the room; she left the door slightly ajar and he could see that she had made changes since he was here the week before. The carpeted hall was now tiled, and there was no artwork on the walls.

"Here, lover." She popped the pill into his mouth and gave him an opened bottle of water to drink. He motioned to the urine bottle on the side table and she took the hint, collected it, and took it into the bathroom while he coughed out his pill and hid it in a lump of croissant.

"Sam, can we talk?" Tom asked.

"Really?" She sat on the bed facing him.

"Yes, really. How did this all go wrong? You and Lucy were friends, we were lovers. How did it all get so angry?"

"I am not angry, Tom—a little hurt, but not angry anymore."

"Then let us go back to how we used to be."

"What about Lucy? She is off the medication now, seeing a different doctor, and hanging with her mum."

"I will leave Lucy. I want to be with you. You know how to treat me. You know what a man wants."

"What about me, Tom? What do I get?"

"Me, me to do your every bidding when and where you want, Sam. I will be your on-call lover. I will never see other women again."

"Forever, Tom, is that what we are talking about? Forever?"

"Yes, if that is what you want, I will give you my forever."

"I don't believe you. Why should I believe you now? You are doing nothing to help me, you never have. Why should I believe you would ever dessert sweet Lucy and be with me?"

"Where am I now, my darling?" He gestured with his one free hand. "Let me make love to you properly with no enhancement, just us being us, like it used to be. Remember that we are so good together."

"What if I said that I do not want to make love to you right now, that I had other things to do?"

"I would say you should do the things that you have to do, and when you come home, you will find me waiting for you, here, your loyal lover."

"You were never my loyal lover."

"I begged to differ. I did not even make love to my wife while we were together."

"Liar."

"I am not a liar."

"No, you won't be loyal to me, not now Lucy thinks she is well. You will want to be with her."

"No, I will not. Untie me. Let me hold you in my arms and show you what you mean to me." She lay in the crook of his arm.

"I want to touch your body, play circles around your belly button while we talk, and play our silly games."

"You mean the silly games where we would discuss all the reasons it would never work between us? Why I did not want you as a husband, how you will always just be a fuck to me because you have nothing else I want?"

"Yes, but with Lucy healthy, I do not have to stay with her anymore, do I? I am free. I can be whatever it is you want me to be for you."

"No, you can't. You are too much a husband, and I do not want a husband."

"Well then, you are in luck because I do not want to be one, I like the idea of being your fuck on call."

"What if I want more?"

"Then I will give it to you. You can take what you want from me." He shook his shackled hand. "Please untie me."

"Not yet." She slid her way down his body, cupping his balls in her hand. She took his cock into her mouth, and it hardened involuntarily, and he watched her. As she watched him watch her, she winked at him, licked the length of his shaft, and took it all into her mouth. He groaned and moved under her as she continued.

Watching her pull her mouth away, his lips parted in anticipation. She straddled him, hovered just over the tip for a moment, and plunged down hard on him, taking all of him inside her. His hips moved to meet her; his one free hand grabbed her breast, squeezing her nipple between his thumb and forefinger the way she liked it.

Her head rolled back, and he felt her come tightening over him. He forced himself to do the same as he looked at her.

"You have never looked at me before. What do you see when you look at me?"

"I see a beautiful, sexy lady that I want to spend eternity with, or as long as she will have me, whatever comes first." He smiled. "Why don't you want to get married? Why don't you want forever?"

"My mum married an Australian. He bought her a house she could clean. After I was born, he paid for my grandparents to come over, as was their deal. He would make her entertain his work colleagues, treat her like a cocktail waitress in a cheap dive bar. She was an doctor. He would threaten to have her deported if she complained. Once he had her dress me up to serve the drinks. She did not like the way he was looking at me and moved me off to my grandparents. She shamed him into letting me go, but he wouldn't let her go."

"That is awful, but she got away. Did she divorce him?"

"No, she killed him accidentally while cleaning her gun."

"She had a gun?"

"Yes, the dumb fuck used to take her shooting. What a mad temptation that must have been for her to just shoot the bastard out in the bush."

"Will you shoot me, Sam?"

"If you want me to? Maybe in the leg or something? I do not want to kill you, Tom. I just want you to do the right thing."

"What is the right thing, Sam? What is it you want me to do?"

"I cannot tell you what it is, Tom. That would be cheating. I can only say at this moment you are closer to doing the right thing than you were this morning, but it is not my job to tell you what to do. Is it?"

"Funny, that is what Lucy always said, too."

"And just who do you think told Lucy?"

She got up and grabbed a knife from the drawer to free his hand from the remaining restraint. Before she could put the knife away, he snatches it. He's hesitant and can't get a hold of her. She was too quick, and he missed the opportunity to stab her. She grabs the blush marble lamp from the nightstand and clocks him over the head with it.

His partially secured body fell into a heap on her, blood from his gash puddled in her cleavage.

"You fuckin' idiot, look what you have made me do. Why can't you just stop being such a fucking wanker?" She slapped him across the head and left.

When he woke, his head was throbbing at the point of impact. He was dressed in disturbingly old-fashioned striped pyjamas, and his hands and feet were cable-tied to the four corners of the bed. His lips felt dry and cracked, and the camera light was on.

She knew he was awake, but he would not ask her for anything. He began counting. You can bear anything for sixty seconds.

On the tenth go around, the door opened, and Sam stepped in, checking his restraints, holding a glass of water with a straw to his mouth, which he took; he did not even ask when she pushed a pill into his mouth, followed by the straw. He dutifully swallowed.

"Good boy," she said. "Later tonight we are going to play, but right now I have people to see, and you will not make a sound, do you understand?" He nods as she leaves.

It did not take long for the room to travel hazily across his eyes, and he was asleep.

LUCY

"Mum, I'm worried. This last text doesn't make sense: *I am going to stay in Perth for work, do not contact me at the house or through work. I need some time away too. Kids are okay.*"

"What is it you dislike, Lucy? The boy has been through a lot, maybe now that he knows you are doing well, the police are on the lookout for Sam and watching us here, the kids are with their other grandparents cruising the Indonesian Archipelago, maybe he just wants some time for himself?"

"This is not how he talks to me on the phone or text, Mum. Something is wrong. I tried to ring him and it goes straight to message bank. I am going to ring his office. Maybe you should, Mum, please, pretend it is something to do with work. They know me, and if he sent these messages and really wants some time to clear his thoughts as he is entitled to after all he has been through, then I will leave it alone."

"After all that he has been through. Lucy, really?"

"Mum, you know what I mean. We were both victims of Sam's games."

"You are way too forgiving. Yes, I said I know you should forgive him, but well, for Christ's sake, Lucy, it is okay to be a little pissed off too. Give me the number."

Sitting on the edge of her chair, Lucy knew that her

mother was right. She should be angry at both Tom and Sam. But she focused her anger on Sam. She was afraid that if she fell down the angry rabbit hole at Tom that she could never forgive him. How do you get back eight years of marriage, eight years of marriage that you lost while you were both living under the same roof, sharing the same bed, raising the same kids, eating the same meals? How could you?

"Well, my love, your instincts were right. Tom is not at work today, and they do not know when they can expect him. She said she knew his wife was ill, so they assumed that his absence has to do with her. Apparently, the boss had said to give him a few days before pestering him for a return date and to just push all his work back as much as possible. We better ring that sergeant what's his name... Always trust your gut, my love."

ANOTHER CAPTIVE

Henry greeted her at the door. She let herself in with the key she collected on her last visit, and the dog followed her through to the kitchen where he begged, whining, next to the treat jar. Sam opened it and passed two treats to the dog, and as she took it, Sam kissed her muzzle.

"You are a good girl, keeping my secret, let's go check on the sitter."

As she was going upstairs, Sam heard the sitter crying. "That will do you no good."

"Hello? Tell me what you want, please if you let me go, I won't tell anyone about you. Just let me take the dog and go."

"Take the dog?" She stood at the door. "You mean steal their dog? What kind of pet sitter are you?" Sam asked.

"I did not mean that I would steal it, just that I would take it away and take care of her until they return from the holiday."

"And what will you say happened? Why did you take the dog? Hmmm, just as I thought. You have not thought it through too well, have you?" said Sam.

"Please, just tell me what you want me to do."

"Enough of the begging, please. You must be thirsty. Hungry perhaps?"

"No, I am fine."

"Really?" Sam asked again.

"Well, maybe a little thirsty?"

"Stay here and I will fetch you something from the kitchen, and then we can talk about what we should do from here."

When Sam returned, she was carrying a tray topped with coffee, a jug of water, a glass, some toast, and biscuits. She untied one of the sitter's hands and both her feet so that she could sit up.

"Thank you," said the sitter.

"It is the least I can do. Tell me, are you due to be looking after any other pets today?"

"No, Henry was it for today."

"Tomorrow?"

"No, just Henry for the entire week."

"Isn't Henry a girl?"

"Yes, they call her Henry, short for Henrietta. What are you doing here? Are you trying to rob them?"

"No, I was looking for my kids. My husband and I have supposedly split up; he left the kids here, and now I find out that they have taken them away. Without asking me, without me saying goodbye to my babies. Who would do such a thing?"

"I had no idea. They seem like such nice people."

"Yes, they do, don't they? You do not know what they are capable of. They want my husband to divorce me and take the children. They say I am no good. They called me an unfit mother. Here, eat your toast." Sam poured the coffee.

"Where is your husband?" the sitter ventured.

"I know where he is, and I know he doesn't have our children. I am worried sick about them. I am sorry I over-reacted when I saw you here. I should not have tied you up like this." She rubbed the sitter's leg.

"Well, now that you have told me what it is all about, I understand. I really do. And like I said, I promise I won't say anything. I can just say that I came here to feed Henry and found the window broken maybe there was someone here, but if nothing is stolen, they would just assume that Henry scared them away and she will be a hero and there would not be an investigation. Nothing stolen, nothing to find or retrieve, hardly a crime at all, just a little damage to an old window."

"You really have thought this through. I am impressed," said Sam.

"Well, you left me here a long time, so I had plenty of thinking time when Henry was not pestering me to rub her belly."

"You have had a lot of time to think it through, to think through how you could trick me."

"No, not trick you. I just want to get out of here, be back home, and forget that this ever happened. Please, you must understand that it is all that I want. To leave here peacefully. I do not want to hurt you. You have been through enough losing your children. I just want to feed Henry and go home. That is all that I came to do." She was sobbed now.

"There, there." Sam patted her leg. "I believe you, but I do not know if I can let you go."

"Please, I know nothing about you, I swear I will tell no

one about you, please, I do not talk to anyone, I live alone, I have no one to share anything with, just my dogs, and they hardly listen to me.. Please let me go."

"No, not yet anyway. I am sorry, but I will have to keep you here until I have done what I set out to do." She reached across and retied the pet sitter's hand to the opposite side of the bedhead.

"Do not make a sound. There is a nanny cam on in this house, and I have the feed on my phone. I will know. Be quiet and show me I can trust you," said Sam.

"I will. You can trust me, oh god, please let me go."

Sam closed the door and left. Henry was close to her side and followed her down to the kitchen. She filled her bowl with biscuits, topped up her water, and left the kitchen door open.

SERGEANT

"The problem we have, Lucy, is that we don't know where Sam is," said Sergeant Leopold.

"I don't understand how she could just disappear," said Lucy.

"Look, I don't know, but is there anywhere you can think of that she, well, you know where she used to meet with Tom?"

"I don't know, Sergeant. I think it was mostly at her place. We have not really had much of a chance to talk about it. You would probably have a better chance of finding out where they went than I would at the moment. Can't you check credit card bills and the like?"

"We have a team working on it, Lucy. Right now, you should just try to rest and let us do our job. We will find him, I promise, and when we do, you will be the first to know."

"Thank you." She hung up the phone. "Well, that was one of the strangest conversations I never want to have again." She turned to her mother sitting at the breakfast bar.

"I think I got the gist of it, sweetheart: they know nothing and hoped that you might know where they used to meet up because that is obviously where she is hiding him. Do they really think that she is hiding him?"

"What do you mean? Do you think he is staying with her deliberately?"

"No, I hope not, anyway. It is just all so strange. I don't understand what her motive is, what is it she wants to achieve from all of this. From where I sit, the gig is up. We know how she manipulated your results, misdiagnosed you, and screwed you up with chemicals. But honestly, why?"

"Because she is fucked in the head, Mum. I know it, you know it, damn, even my stupid husband has come to the realisation. It doesn't make sense because there is none. No motive, nothing. I have been putting up with her and her bullshit for years, and she just kept pushing me, bullying me, manipulating me into doing whatever she wanted me to do. We were not friends. I was always her experiment."

"I am sorry, Lucy, I should have put a stop to your friendship years ago, before it destroyed you. I knew Sam was trouble."

"I bet even you could never have guessed just how fucked up she is. Who could of suspected all this?"

TOM

Tom stirred, drowsy from the medication she fed him. He felt the pressure of her body on the end of the bed. Her hand was running up and down his leg.

"Sam, what are you doing?"

"I am trying to decide what to do. It seems no one is missing you. Your children are on a cruise with Nanny and Pop, and your wife is too busy getting her life back together to care about what you are up to. Do you think she already knows about us?"

"I don't know. Maybe. She doesn't have to care about me knowing what we did to her," said Tom.

"Yes, it was not very nice what we did to her. You have been a very, very bad husband. You do not deserve to be married to beautiful, sweet, and innocent Lucy. You are not worthy of such a prize."

"Is this what I deserve? To be tied up here, no free will, waiting for you to come in here, drug me, feed me, let me go to the toilet, fuck me, film me, keeping me helpless? You do not have to do this, Sam. I understand now that we belong together."

"Shut up. You are just trying to trick me."

"No, I see it now. None of us deserves Lucy. We both tried to destroy her. Doesn't that show that we do not even love her, we just played with her all these years? From that first night I fucked you in Bali, I knew we were meant to be together—you were on fire, hot, passionate, terrifying, and I wanted more. I should have done more for Lucy, taken her to someone else, but you captured me, still. You do not need this. You don't need straps and drugs to keep me here. I have and will always be under you spell."

"Words, Tom, they are just empty words. You have done nothing for me."

"That is not fair, Sam. You have never asked me. You told me not to leave Lucy. She was too unstable, that we could carry on as we were. Lucy is not unstable anymore. We can be lovers now, we can be everything to each other now. I don't need to stay."

"You realise that there is a good chance I am going to prison for malpractice?" said Sam.

"Yes, but I will be there. We can have conjugal visits." He winked at her. "And I will wait for you when you get out early for good behaviour."

"Then what? They will ruin me."

"You won't have to work. I will take care of you. We can move away, change our names and party until we are too old to care."

She stood up. "Bullshit, Tom, it is more of your bullshit."

"I swear to you, Sam, I mean every word I say. Tell me what to do to prove it to you."

She said nothing as she pushed the straw into his mouth, followed by another red pill, and left the room.

Sam maneuvered through the boxes that were scattered around the house. In the library, she stopped, opened a box labelled with a capital A, grabbed some books, and neatly arranged them on the wooden shelves in alphabetical order.

His words ran through her head. What was she going to do with him now?

THE FAT MAN

The sitter could hear the footsteps on the stairs and the sound of paws trotting after them. Thinking it must be Sam, so she didn't cry out. She wanted Sam to know that she could trust her if she let her go. It surprised the sitter to see Ged, the fat man in the leather pants, standing at the opened door.

"Hello, dear, do not be alarmed. Sam sent me to take care of you."

"What do you mean, take care of me? Is Sam not coming back? She said that she would come back."

"Later maybe, but how about you and me get to know each other a little first?" He sat on the bed. His weight caused her to involuntarily roll towards him.

"That's the idea," he said, putting his hand on her hip and running it down the length of her leg. "Are you comfortable, dear?"

"No, not really. Could you untie me? I could really use the bathroom and, oddly, a drink." She tried to cover the shake in her voice.

"Seems fair enough. I guess you have been here a long time."

"Since yesterday."

He reached across her so that his armpit is directly above her face and untied her restraints.

"Thank you."

"You are welcome." He took hold of a hand and pulled her up off the bed, bringing her to stand before him. He looked her in the eye; they were the same height.

"You are kind of cute, I guess, sweet even." He walked her to the bathroom and refused to leave her.

"If you have to stay, please at least be a gentleman and turn around,"

"You and I both know that I am no gentleman."

When she finished and went to pull up her pants, but he grabbed her arm. "There is no need for pants. In fact, I guess you could use a shower, couldn't you? I am going to watch you, okay? Now take off your shirt."

"Please, do not hurt me, I will tell no one anything. Just please let me go."

"I will not hurt you, I am going to pleasure you in a way you have never been pleasured before, I imagine so anyway, so please do not keep me waiting. It makes me impatient, and if I get impatient, I am likely to forget my manners."

She unbuttoned her shirt, folded it and sat it on the bathroom vanity, leaving her naked now but for her white, plain, cotton bra.

"Jesus, where to you buy this stuff, Sexless Express?" He chuckled. "Take it off and show me your tits."

The sitter struggled to hold back a sob as she obeyed him.

"Get in the shower. I want none of your crying shit, it makes my little dick go soft."

She stepped into the shower and set the water.

"Wash yourself with that soap. I want you to smell nice for me."

She turned her back to him.

"I want you to turn around and wash that pussy of yours. Do not turn away from me again, Sam promised me we could play, and that is exactly what I intend to do."

"Sam told you to come here?"

"Yes, yes, she did. She told me she did not know what to do with you, so that I was free to do with you anything I wanted in return for a small job that she needed me to do."

"What job?"

"Just a little trip to Albany, not really any of your business. Wash under your tits."

"Sorry, I just feel so self-conscious of you standing there watching me, I forgot my place."

"Fair enough. Do not let it happen again. You are not here to question me. You are here to do what I tell you, everything that I told you to do. Okay?"

"Yes, sir."

"That is better. Now rinse off and dry yourself. Slowly."

She did as instructed, stepped out of the shower, took a towel from the rack, looking at him the whole time. She forced eye contact. She knew it was best to be compliant.

He took her by the hand and led her back to the bedroom. He laid her lie down on the bed, positioned her arms and leg wide to the corners, and he tied her there.

Looking into her face, he lost his will. She had no fight in her. She was not his type, and he was not horny now; she was older, her belly soft and the veins on her legs showed. He didn't want to hurt her. He didn't want to push his little cock inside her crow-lined mouth, or even up her soft, cellulite arse. He just did not want to. He left the room with the door ajar, patted the dog, and left the house. In the driveway, he texted Sam. *Na, mate, that is not my type, left naked on the bed, you go fuck her! Then find another way to pay me.*

When Sam saw the text, it disappointed her. Fat man could have solved his sitter problem. His tendency to violence could have gotten rid of her properly, and she would be free. *Fuck it*, she thought. What was she going to do with her now? Lying there waiting for the fat man, and he didn't want it. Fuck, that was a blow to a girl's self-esteem.

It was dark when Sam reached the house. Standing at the door to the room, she saw the sitter was asleep. She tiptoed to the bed, the light coming through the window striped across her body, her skin a landscape of goose bumps. In the evening light, she might be attractive. Sam pulled out her phone and took a shot, sent it the fat man with the tag, *how about now?*

Nothing.

She could smell the musk of her. "Someone should want you, someone should be prepared to make you feel special," Sam whispered in the darkness, and she slid her fingertips along the length of the sitter's inside leg, past her knee and into her slit.

The sitter groaned, her hips rising slightly, and it took Sam in. She slipped off her shoes and used her mouth along the inside of the sitter's thigh. She used her fingers to part her lips and drove her tongue in hard.

The sitter stirred, her hips rose, and consciousness stirred her. She became aware of the room, the tongue on her clit, the scent of her, not him. Her eyes were closed, and she played asleep. This could be a dream like many others that she had had in the past, sleeping alone on a hot summer night with a cool breeze blowing the curtains across her room. She let out a groan as Sam inserted a finger into her, coaxing her to take two, then three fingers.

Sam caressed her with her tongue, willing the sitter to come. Her own pants were getting wet, and she wanted the sitter to touch her in the darkness. She moved her face to the sitter's.

"Wake up. Let's have some fun. We are going to sixty-nine." Sam stood up, pulled her dress over her head, pushed her knickers to the floor and stood there naked.

The sitter watched Sam in the moonlight and aches to be touched.

Sam straddled the sitter's face and lowered herself down. She responded instantly and dove her tongue in and around the labia to bring Sam's clit to a climax.

Sam lowered her chest across the sitter's belly and worked her pussy, loving the salty tang of her, willing her to come. Sam changed position to kiss the sitter's mouth and share the taste of her.

"Untie my hands, please let me touch you."

Sam sat upright, straddling the sitter, staring down at her in the moonlit room. "You are quite beautiful. I would have never picked that you are gay. I guess fat man did, and

that is why he left you alone."

"I am not gay. I have never been with a woman before, but you are amazing."

"Are you sure?"

"Yes, honest, check out my pathetic tinder profile, prefers men! Geez, did I get that wrong?"

"Maybe you are bi?"

"Do you think that is possible? Please untie me, one hand even, I want to touch you."

Sam was turned on by the sincerity in the sitter's eyes. She released one hand, and as she straddled the sitter to kiss her mouth, the sitter's hand explored Sam's body.

When Sam turned again to sit on her face, the sitter used her hands with her tongue and brought Sam to a climax.

Sam lay at her side. "You did not come?"

"I never do. I think my pussy is broken. I have never been with a man, woman, or toy that made me climax. I just never get there. I have tried everything from mirrors, jade eggs, tantra, twenty-seven different vibrators, and shagging fresh produce, and nothing. My cunt is broken."

"Maybe I can help you with that."

"Really, that would be cool, but I don't know how."

"I know some things."

"I know, I have seen, but I am not sure that it will be enough. I mean, you are sexy and that was hot, licking a woman, touching you inside, feeling your breasts, that was something else, but while it feels good, there are no contractions, no spasms, no come shooting out like on the films."

"I can help. I am a therapist, would you believe?"

"I know, and you are not their daughter-in-law, and I do not know what your game is, but I want more of you, more exploration, to find out more about you. Do not even let me go until you are done. Just say that we can have more of this, playing around together. This is truly the most amazing thing that has ever happened to me."

"Shut up. You cannot be serious. Can you seriously be so starved for love and affection that you would fall for me? You are not even gay. I sent the fat man to rape you, knowing full well that he would probably kill you."

"I know he told me all that, but he didn't, and you came and came, and we have something going on here and I dare you to deny it. We were meant to be together and you know it. That is why I am still here."

"I could have you killed," said Sam.

"Yes, you could, but you won't because you feel it too."

"You don't know what I feel. You think that because I had an orgasm that we are something, that we are meant to be together, that we are it now, that we are going to go on fucking even when I eventually get out of jail? Do not look at me like that."

"Like what?"

"Like you think it is hot that I am going to jail, and we will be fucking! We might be, but I am going to have to teach you some things, like how to come. I find it very disconcerting that you didn't. We have to fix that first, then we will work on your Stockholm syndrome."

LUCY

Lucy sat across from the doctor.

"Tell me about your husband."

"Tom? What do you want to know? He is a nice man, good job, and a great father."

"What is he like as your husband? Not what you say to distance relatives or write on a gravestone. What is he like as your husband?"

"I do not know what you want me to say."

"Okay, let me see if I can make it a little less broad. Tell me about when you first showed signs that something wasn't okay after the babies, that you were having a hard time. How did Tom take care of you?"

"I don't know. He told me I was acting strange and that I should see a doctor. That I probably needed some pills or something."

"Did he give you some time away from the baby or suggest that the two of you do something together?"

"You mean like a date night?"

"Yes."

"I suggested a date night, but he said we couldn't afford to go out and hire a sitter, but if I wanted to get a sitter during the day while he was at work, I could go something nice for myself."

"Did he suggest anything?"

"You know, girl stuff, get my legs waxed or something."

"Why didn't he offer to look after the babies so that you could do something?"

"Because he spent all his time at work. Even when he had the flu, he would go to work. He would say because someone has to, we need the money. I guess we need money more than we needed to spend any time together from how he saw things, anyway. I remember one day he had food poisoning so bad, but he had to be at work at a particular time, anyway. He obviously had diarrhea and was vomiting and got caught without a bucket on the toilet and threw up all over the toilet floor. He woke me and said, *Sorry, I left a mess in the toilet.* When I went to see, confused, tired, and needing to go to the toilet as you do when you first wake up, he had laid a towel all over his spew. It was splashed up the wall and the outside of the bowl. We only had one toilet. I had to go outside to pee, then came back to clean it up before the babies woke."

"How did that make you feel?"

"Like a low grade servant, but I cleaned it up and disinfected the entire room, threw the towel in the bin, and rang him to see if he was okay."

"Was he?"

"No, he said that he felt like shit, but had to be at work. Then when I questioned why, he yelled at me, said I didn't understand where the money coming from, and so on."

"What about when he came home from work that night? Did he apologise?"

"No, but he must have been feeling better because he still went to the gym that night. He went most days of the week."

"How did that make you feel?"

"I wanted the babies. He wanted to be fit. I figured he would spend time with me when he wanted. I did not want to stand in his way of getting what he wanted. He always worked so hard. You don't treat people like that. It isn't fair."

"But what about what you wanted?"

"I didn't want much, just a family. I wanted him to support me and to help me in raising that family. I didn't really want anything for myself. I was tired from looking after the babies, but I just wanted time together, to know that he was happy and to be with him. You know, the life in the pram ads, couples together forever, happy Kodak memories. But he would not even take time from work for a photo shoot. I won a family photo shoot at a raffle and he could not take the time off work to come along. It was only for an hour."

"How did it make you feel?"

"Second best, always second best, less important and not worth time. Always finding ways to be useful, to be important, to be put first and never being important enough to be first, until..."

"Until when?"

"Bedtime. He wanted sex and pushed up behind me like I should wipe away the day and be grateful that I have his full attention, that I was important now. That now he wanted to make me happy and if I do not let him, then it is obviously because I have something wrong with me. But the whole time it was just the end of a long train of disappointments, of being put last. And it doesn't feel that it and by "it" I mean having sex with him—has anything to do with making me happy and everything to do with making him happy, because maybe if he really wanted to make me happy he would start by spending time with me and not just taking from me, then complain that he did not get his fair share, that I rejected him when there is a whole line of rejections on my list that I had to contend with. Sorry, I don't know where that came from."

"Did you feel loved?"

"No."

"Do you think you withheld sex from Tom deliberately?"

Yes, I did. In the beginning, being ignored is not a turn on. Being put second is not a turn on."

HUNTING TOM

"Mum, I am going. You can't talk me out of this. I do not care what the sergeant said, I don't think Sam will hurt me. I have to find out where Tom is, and she is keeping him somewhere. I know she is."

"Lucy, what if she isn't?"

"What do you mean?"

"You know what I mean. What if Tom is with her voluntarily?"

"What if Tom has left me for her after all these years of pretending to stand by me?"

"Yes."

"Mum, he could not have known what she was doing. Why would he or anyone else go along with that? If he was unhappy, he could have left. I would not have gone after his money. What money? There is nothing to be financially gained from staying married. He is not an overly involved father, so he hasn't stayed with me for fear of losing of the kids—I wouldn't do that to him anyway, nevertheless, that is not why he stayed."

"Guilt?"

"Maybe? But like he reminds me often, I wanted the children more, so why should he feel guilty? He could be a really crappy husband, but mostly I believe he loves me, and if he doesn't, then I need to find out and get things sorted before the kids come home. Mum, if he doesn't want to be with me, if he wants to run away with Sam or that big-titted receptionist at his office, then I want to know, and I want him to piss off so I can get cracking on my life."

"And if he is not leaving you, are you going to make sure that you get what you want?"

"You bet I am, Mum. No more apologising for being broken. I am standing tall and taking my life back. My doctor will help me find someone near home, since he thinks I will need to continue counselling for some time, but I can do it. I can get past this, Mum."

Izzy held her arms out wide for a hug. "Of course, you can, my darling." She squeezed her daughter close. "That is my clever girl. You are going to be just fine. You know I am always here to help you, take care of you, whatever you need, beautiful. I will come with you."

"No, you can't. You have to watch the Jones family menageries. This is your livelihood, how you get on with doing the life you want, the life you deserve. I really believe that Sam doesn't intend to hurt me physically, and she can no longer touch me mentally. I will stay in touch. I may need you to keep Sergeant Leopold informed. I think he enjoys talking to you."

"Lucy, really? No, I have no time for such things."

"You should always make time for love, Mum."

"Seriously, Lucy, you are too much."

"I am. Mum, can I borrow your car?"

"Of course. The keys are in the ignition. I can use the Joneses" family car, it is in the contract."

FREMANTLE

Lucy arrived back at her home in Fremantle just after lunch. Letting herself in the front door, she pushed past the mail collected on the floor, and she saw his handprint pressed into the rug. His watch and keys were in the bowl in the hall. She headed up the stairs to the bedroom. The sheets were rumpled, pretty much the way she left it. She tidied the bed and noticed his smell was on her pillow. She smiled. He must have missed her. Maybe he had even been thinking about her. Perhaps there was still a chance for their marriage.

His towel was on the bathroom floor, hair in the sink. *This is marriage,* she thought. His clothes were on top of the washing basket, the same as always. Even in her absence, there was comfort in routine.

Lucy moved through to his office. She sat at his desk and, opening the top drawer, she found tickets, receipts for flowers that she never received, a catalogue from Victoria's Secret with some ticks amongst the pages, things that she knew nothing about. Last Christmas, he gave her a pair of car seat covers. These gifts were not for her. They must have been for Sam.

She scanned through his diary for signs, but there was nothing. These gifts were a sign that he thought of Sam, but nothing to suggest that he was in love with her. How would she know without the chance to speak to him? Lucy would have to keep assuming that it was lust, manipulated lust, and that her husband loved her, and that he wanted to be found and he wanted to come home, that there was a future for them and their family that Sam did not exist in.

Lucy took a shower, then dressed in black pants, black top, and black hiking books. She grabbed a set of mini screwdrivers and a hammer from the garage before driving Tom's Ute the short distance to Sam's family home.

The house had been deserted long ago. An overgrown garden surrounded by a temporary cyclone fence around the perimeter to give the feeling that it was about to join other houses in the Mosman Park street to be gutted, torn down, and renovated. With Tom's clipboard in hand, she squeezed her way through the fence and waded through the weeds towards the house. She walked around acting like a surveyor, and when she was sure that no one was watching, she pulled the hammer from her back pocket and with a swift hit, she broke the laundry window and pushed her arm through the hole to open the door.

The house was just as she remembered it on that dreadful night when Sam's grandmother was found dead, right down to the police tape and chalk outline on the kitchen floor. The fridge hummed, and despite herself she opened the door; mould and sourness putrefied the air.

She remembered the old lady in the lounge room, her slippers on the floor next to her recliner, the tray that sat across her lap, the crossword, the sudoku, the games one uses to keep their minds alive, but what for? She was gone without ever properly reaching old age, without ever losing her faculties.

Lucy passed the bedroom where the sheets were turned down, a glass of water still on the bedside table. Past the study and into the room that used to be Sam's, when she was growing up and sometimes as a refuge when adult life got too hard. It looked to be disturbed; the dust on the door had been wiped, inside some books had been pulled, leaving a dust map on the shelf and the bed where they had been placed.

In the desk drawers she found notebooks from school. Lucy scanned through the pages, mostly familiar; some in English, some in Mandarin; there were drawings, some of her and Sam, her mum, her grandparents, juvenile, teen girl fantasies, houses, money, cars, fashion clips; Madonna on the wall, nothing to say why she became Sam, where the mean streak came, the quest for possessing things and people. Other people's people particularly.

The study, once meticulously kept by Sam's grandfather, had evolved into stacks after his death, layers of information by her grandmother.

A HOMECOMING

When the sitter woke, she was dressed in silk pyjamas. The smell of bacon oozed into the room, a pan sizzling, coffee in the air. She did not want to move. She felt the weight of Henry's body on the bed next to her leg. It was like waking up to a lover and being treated like a goddess; it had happened once before, and it made her heart flutter. She was unsure of what to do. Should she get up? Wait?

"Hello?" she called out into the smells.

"Oh, hello dear," came the familiar voice, and Tom's mum appeared at the door. "Well, how are we doing there, Miss Goldilocks?" she laughed. "So sorry you had to go to so much trouble and spend the night here. We got a call just as we landed in the port of Langkawi that the house had been broken into and you had stopped them. It must have been terrifying! Anyway, the locksmith has been and fixed the lock, and the glacier came to fix the window. Honestly, we are so very grateful that you stayed overnight."

"Oh, um, it was no problem at all. I wanted to see that Henry was safe."

"Here you go." Tom's dad put the breakfast tray on the bed beside her. "Especially for our hero."

A bag she did not bring from home was on the chair

next to the bed, and she recognised her clothes folded on top.

"Thank you."

"You look pale. Take all the time you need, get some rest, and eat something. Honestly, you are welcome to stay as long as you like," said Tom's mother.

"Thank you, but now that you are home, I really need to get back home. How was your trip?"

"Well, I do not think we will take another cruise anytime soon. Gastro went through the entire ship for the first few days, which wasn't pretty, as you can imagine. Bad enough we were ill, but sharing with two kids as well, well, that was tough. A lot of the staff were ill so there was not much help. It was a full-on misery ship. We had travel insurance, but there was not enough medicine to go around. Within the first forty-eight hours, it had to be flown in and dropped by helicopter."

"Sounds awful," the sitter consoled, "and then to come home to this."

"Oh, this is nothing. I am just glad that you were not hurt. I think the police may want to speak to you at some stage. Here I have a card." She handed the sitter the card from Sergeant Leopold.

Johah and Marty ran into the room, jumping on the bed to fuss over Henry. "Let's take Henry for a walk, Nanna, come on to the park, please."

"Oh, of course I think that is a good idea, it will give our sitter a chance to get some rest."

"Thank you, but if you do not mind, I would really like to get home. Thank you for all your help."

"No trouble at all. Thank you. We owe you the world for keeping our Henry safe."

"That is my job and my pleasure." She scuffed the dog's head as they left. She listened for the clatter to turn to silence when the front door closed. She counted to ten, got out of bed, grabbed her bag, and drove past the family walking the dog a few minutes later.

SAM

Tom's phone rang in Sam's bag and startled her as she watched the departure from across the street. She waited a safe time before following the pet sitter as she weaved through the suburban streets on her way home.

"Well, that was a quick getaway. Still in the pyjamas I put you in, I see," said Sam.

"Thank you. How did you know they were coming home?"

"I didn't, I did that because I wanted you to feel comfortable, to know that I don't intend to harm you," said Sam.

"What happened?"

"I was coming back to see you, to let you go, to tell you to go home. I want to spend more time with you," said Sam.

"Why?"

"To explore, to see where we could go, if there is something here. I haven't been able to stop thinking about you," said Sam.

"Sam, I have had no time to think. You drugged me, tried to get me raped, drugged me, made love to me, left me tied to a bed in a client's home... thankfully you dressed me and untied me just before the family came home. For that, I am grateful, but I do not know what else I feel right now. I just want to go into my home, take a shower and do nothing. I do not want to think about anything right now, not you, and certainly not the fat man."

Sam reached her arms out. "Can I trust you, pet sitter? I need to know. I am up to my ears in shit here and I would like to know that I can trust you and that we will be okay, and maybe you will let me buy you dinner soon. Tonight maybe?"

"Sam, as tempting as that is, and sadly it is the best offer that I have had in a long time. I am free now. I am not tied up to a bed, I am free to choose, and I think I choose to say

no. You have a lot of shit to sort out, don't you?"

"Maybe, but what if I don't? What if, I just send Tom back to his wife, lie low for a while, and make myself available to you? We could spend time together getting to know each other if you want to?"

"I would like that very much, but I do not want to start something amid all this mess that you created. I find you to be intriguing, but dangerous. I am not sure that I am strong enough for a relationship with you, Sam."

"I wouldn't hurt you, I promise," said Sam.

"Really, is that what you told Tom?"

"Tom is different. He asked to have an affair with me. He neglected his wife. He used me. This time, this punishment he is undergoing is just his karma catching up with him," said Sam.

"For using you or for cheating on his wife? Aren't you two friends?"

"Since school," said Sam.

"What about you? Don't you think you deserve some comeuppance for cheating on her with him? It is a shitty thing to do, don't you think? You were friends and a doctor, and I guess she trusted you."

"Shut up. You know nothing about it."

"Then tell me, Sam, help me understand why you did that to your friend. I want to understand why you did what you did and what is different between us that makes it true that you do not intend to do the same to me. I do not want to be hurt. I want to know that this is not who you are. Tell me who you are, Sam. Show me what kind of woman you really are."

"How do you intend I do that?"

"Well, for starters, come in. I am going to make you a cup of tea, maybe some lunch, and we can talk."

"I don't know how long I can stay," said Sam.

Sam went after her into the house. The jarrah floorboards were glossed, and the walls in the hall were covered in pictures of her own golden retriever. A photo of her and the dog as a puppy was next to an urn on a small table.

"Where is Tom?"

"Tied to my bed. I gave him a sedative before I left, so he will be out for a few more hours at least," said Sam.

"Are you worried that he would make a noise and be heard by your neighbours?" They stood together in the kitchen. Sam watched as she filled the kettle and put it on the burner. She grabbed two cups from the top cabinets and put them on a tray with a teapot, sugar bowl, and spoon.

"No, he is nowhere near anyone. My house is built in such a way that from the inside, it looks just like my last house, but it is contained," said Sam.

"Like your last house, that is unusual." She moved to the fridge, took out a carton of milk and smelt the contains. She filled the small ceramic cow shaped just and added it to the tray.

"I liked my house. I wanted the same, just in a different area," said Sam.

"Are you far from here? Is it easy for you to get here from there?" She opened a packet of bakers muffins and sat two on the tray.

"It is not too bad. Why all the questions?"

"I told you, I am trying to understand who you are and why you are doing what you are doing." She pulled the kettle from the head at the first sign of the whistle and filled the teapot.

"Why?"

"Because I need to believe that you are a decent person, that you are just caught up in this extraordinary situation." She took the tray to the living room. They were seated opposite each other, with the tray resting on the coffee table between them.

"I created this situation. I am not a victim; I am the creator." Sam sat forward on her chair and poured the tea into both mugs.

"I know, but why? That is exactly what I want to know."

"Do you think I am an evil woman? Here." Sam handed her a cup of tea and offers her a muffin from the tray.

"No—well, at least, I am willing to discover either way."

"Are you not afraid that I may hurt you?"

"Are you going to call the fat man again?"

"No, I promise."

"Is there someone worse?"

"No, there is just me, confused me."

"What is confusing you?"

"You are? What are you doing? You should call the police. You know I trapped Tom at my house. I imprisoned you. I would have the fat man rape you. He would have beat you up good too. He likes to do that to women."

"Why didn't he then?"

"Honestly, he said it was because of the lines around your mouth. He saw them while you were sleeping. They intrigued me when I saw them. He said that you were too old. He wanted young things, not old. I am sorry. I didn't see you that way."

"What do you see when you look at me?"

"Kindness, love, and a hot body."

"Do not go there now. Tell me what makes you think we might have something."

"You looked at me," sighed Sam.

"You looked at me too."

"I think I may have seen you, who you are." Sam leaned forward to kiss her.

"I think that I may have seen who you are too, but I want to learn more about you, so I would rather you did not distract me with your sexy lips and wily ways."

"Wily ways?"

"Yes, Sam, seriously, I want to talk to find out about who you are. Sex will not be enough to keep us together in the future. I will help you finish what you have started, Sam. I will even look after you while you are on the lam, but you must show me who you are."

"I can't, not really, not everything. You would not like me if you knew everything that there is to know about me."

"You do not know that. You do not know me. But if you are so afraid, leave out the worst."

"I was not expecting this. I thought you would hate me, attack me, call the police, do something, anything, anything but be nice to me. I do not deserve this. I do not deserve you. What is your name? I cannot keep calling you the pet sitter."

"Toni."

"Tony?"

"Toni with an I."

"Okay. Toni, I am open. I am prepared to answer all your questions, honestly, within the limits of keeping the worst to myself."

"Okay then let us start early. Where were you born?"

"China. We came out here when I was three years old, my mother, my father, and me. My father was an Australian, my mother was a doctor. She helped him with his drug addiction, and she ran a recovery program somewhere in China. They were married and then he brought us here."

"What was he like? Your father."

"I don't know. They divorced when I was six years old. He was a drug-addicted musician, my mum the doctor could not be with him, so we went to live with my grand-parents in Mosman Park."

"What was your mother like?"

"She would disappear a lot for work, but as I got older, I worked out that it was something else. If it was for work, I am sure my grandparents would not have argued with her so much. I remember now that one time all my mother's photos were taken down. Gone. It was like she never existed. My grandmother said she brought shame to the ancestors."

"What were they like with you?"

"Strict, really strict. I couldn't go anywhere. Finally, in year six, I had to spend time at Lucy's house to do home-work. Both my grandparents would wait outside of Lucy's house, out there on the sidewalk. My grandfather died out there on the sidewalk waiting for me to supposedly finish a project on Australian history."

"That was not your fault."

"Yes, it was. There was no project, it was just a way of getting to spend time at Lucy's house."

"Why did you want to spend so much time there?"

"Lucy's family were awesome. Their house was loud, colourful, her brother was gay, and that caused a lot of arguments between her mum and dad and her dad and George. He is lovely, you would like him; he was tall, blonde, handsome."

"Did you like him?"

"I just told you he was gay."

"Doesn't mean that you did not like him. Besides, you already told me you were bi."

"I am tired, Toni."

"Would you like to rest?" She stood up and held out her hand to Sam. Come on, we can rest, we can lie down together and rest, just for a little while. Then when you wake, you will know what to do with Tom."

"Will you stay with me, Toni?"

"Of course." Toni led the way down her the hallway to her bedroom. She threw some cushions off the bed; they scattered along the floor. She laid Sam down on the bed, taking off her shoes and letting them drop to the floor. Toni walked around the bed and spooned in behind Sam, wrapping her arms around her waist, pressing her face into the space between her shoulder blades. They closed their eyes and allowed themselves to rest.

TOM

Tom woke up on the bed, face down and with arms and legs stretched out. He was bound by his hands and feet to the bed's corners. His mouth was silenced with a gag. Someone ran scissors up the length of his pyjamas top. He could feel the cold liquid as it was poured onto his skin. A knife cut into him. Sawing away at his skin. His screams were muffled. The restraints on his wrists and ankles held him firm to the bed. Helpless, he passed out long before the pushing and tugging stopped.

Next time he woke, the bed was wet. He could smell his own blood staining the sheets. There was a pain in his side, his hands and feet were freed. Tom inched his body up to sitting. He cried out loud, the pain unbearable. He staggered up and made his way to the bathroom. He threw up in the sink, looked down at his blood-stained torso. In the mirror he could see the stitches that arced around his back and torso. "What the fuck?"

On the vanity were two bottles of tablets, with "Take two" and "Take one" written on the labels. He obeyed the instructions, pouring himself a glass of water and swallowing the pills. His head was spinning. He found the door out of the room, pulled his way along the boxes down the hall towards the front door. He reaches for the door handle, but it was double locked from the outside.

It wouldn't open. He slid to the floor in a heap against it.
Blackness.

LUCY

Lucy pulled a red velvet shoe box from under Sam's bed, wiped a layer of dust from its top, and put the lid to her side. Pulling out the first folded piece of paper, she found a letter Sam had written to herself in seventh grade. It was for a class project where everyone had to send a letter to their future self. Sam had been determined that she was going to get it right and inspire her future self to not be a dweeb.

Dear Sam,

You are an idiot and you will always be an idiot and it does not matter what you did at university or how many times that you did not get caught breaking the law you are an idiot if you do not marry Lucy and find a way of having babies. Think about how cool it will be to marry your best friend. Look around you now, Sam, you are in a beautiful house that you share with your husband, yes I know I said that you are going to marry Lucy but you realise you want burritos more than tacos, so you leave her for a handsome, interesting man with a high paying job and give Lucy the kids because she would be better with them than you ever could be because her mother is not a total complete bitch loser that doesn't deserve to walk the face of this earth.

Anyway, remember Sam, you are smart and capable of doing anything. Do not let this Chinese-Australian gig get in your way forever. You be the best doctor you can be! And shut down that stupid Asian whore house slave market your family runs from the Fremantle warehouse. You don't owe them nothing.

Lucy held a photo she remembered her mother taking of them both just before their grade seven Christmas concert. Such an easier time then. They were smiling at the camera in her mother's house, and George was in the background at his piano, practising. Lucy scanned the other photos of Sam's parents, her grandparents, the feathered dart her grandmother pulled from her neck the day she died.

She returns the book to its place under the bed with the contents intact except for the photo of two young girls in Christmas dresses. She slips that into her back pocket. Moving through the house and on to the study, she scoured the bookcases that lined the walls. According to Sam, there was a safe somewhere. *Where would someone hide a safe?* She fingered the dust along the bookcases: Chinese, leather bound, Australian law books, cookbooks along the bottom. They were collectors. They would hunt through garage sales and flea markets looking for things. They were constantly chasing Australian culture, trying to build something around their granddaughter that was separate from their own.

Lucy heard a thud in the kitchen, too hard for a cat or bird, and she realised she left the kitchen door unlocked. Crouching on all fours, she crawled on hands and knees to the back of the desk, hoping the vanity screen would hide her.

She heard a hissing, "Lucy... Lucy..."

She knew the voice. "Mum!"

"Yes, Lucy, where are you?"

Lucy stood up, banging her head on the standard lamp. "Mum! What are you doing here?"

"I have come to help, come to see that you do not get yourself into any more trouble, and because something exciting is going on and I want in."

"How did you know I would be here?"

"I didn't, really. I went to your place first, then it occurred to me when you were not at the Dome where I had to grab a coffee that you might give this old place a go. What have you found out?"

"Nothing really, except Sam is a hoarder. This is her grandfather's study. I figured that there must be something in here, a clue to something. I'm glad you are here, Mum, this place is creeping me out some."

"Yes, I can see why it would. Let's get into it." She

pulled open a desk draw and pulled out the first file. "Interesting," said Izzy.

"What is?"

"Did you know the Halong's were importer exporters?"

"No, I didn't know what they did. I always thought the only thing that her grandparents did was make her life miserable and stop her from being an Australian. Then I see all these books on Australia that they must have collected. There are literally hundreds of them on all sorts of topics."

"Maybe they were just trying to understand? You know, for Sam's sake," said Isabel.

"They seemed to warm to you, eventually. Remember how they used to stand outside of our house waiting for her when she came to our house to do homework with you? Like they were expecting her to try to run away or something."

"Or something," said Lucy.

"Or something? What do you mean? Look at this, it is a list of names, I think. Here, you studied Mandarin in at school, what does this say?"

"It looks like a list of names. Here, this means arrived, paid, and these are numbers. This character means *ship*."

"Oh, Lucy, are you thinking what I am thinking?" "Probably not," said Lucy.

"Names, a list, money, a ship—those old goats were smugglers."

"Smugglers? Smuggling what?"

"Probably all sorts of things from China. How do you think Fremantle markets got started?"

"Illegal imports? I would have thought more like handicrafts."

"Good god, girl, even handicrafts need raw materials, plastic beads, bells and the like. Everything is made in China, well, everything that they cannot palm off to the Indians."

"Mum!"

"Well it is true, dear, chances are that your precious designer t-shirt costs two dollars in Bangladesh! Lucy, look, there are hundreds of these."

"Mum, there is too much for me to decipher. I only remember a bit from school."

"I know who can help," said Isabel.

"Who?"

"George. He was a translator to the Australian consulate in China."

"Yes, and we are both very proud of him but we cannot get him involved in this, we can't tell him we have broken into Sam's grandparents' house looking for clues as to where she is, where she is keeping Tom, and what the heck we plan to do with her when we find this all out!"

"Okay, then who?" Izzy asked, hand on hip.

"I do not know but keep looking. Maybe there is something in English that will help us?"

Lucy ploughed through a stack of papers in a desk drawer. "Look, what is this, Mum?" Lucy pulled another manilla folder out of the desk drawer. "This full of invoices, from builders and tradesmen, recently billed."

"Is there an address?" said Izzy.

"Yes, look on Peter Hughes Drive, along the warehouse strip." said Lucy.

"The cheeky buggers, right near Fremantle harbour. I bet they know where Sam is," said Isabel.

"She could be keeping Tom there. We should call the Sergeant, let him know what we found." said Lucy.

"Yes." Isabel pulled her mobile from her back pocket and dialled the sergeant.

SAM

Sam could feel the warm breath breezing into the arch at the back of her neck. Toni's arms were around her waist, in the darkened room. They were still in the same position that they laid down in. Nothing but the light in the room had changed.

"You should go," came Toni's voice from behind her.

"I don't want to," said Sam.

"He may need you."

"He could escape if he wanted to."

"But he could go straight to the police."

"They don't know where to find me."

"No, but you could never go home again, and never put a stop to this madness. Always be on the run, afraid to live your life. Seriously, I bet he won't press charges."

"It is not just Tom, Toni." She turned into her arms to lay face to face.

"Then what?"

"What I did to Lucy."

"Why did you do that? Lucy was your friend," said Toni.

"I don't know, except that I wanted to control her. I wanted to hang onto her. My family was powerful—secretly powerful, but powerful all the same. No one suspected the life my grandparents led. They looked so sweet, innocent, dumb naïve immigrants, when in fact they controlled millions of dollars of, black market trade."

"But, Sam, what about Lucy? Why did you want to control her?"

"Because that is what my people do. Do you hate me?"

"No, I am trying to understand you. You excite me, you make me want to learn more about you, but how do I know you are not playing a game with me, like you did with Lucy?"

"Because I didn't want you. I was going to have you raped and left for dead. I didn't care about you. I didn't care enough about you. I didn't plan to control you. I never wanted to. There was no reason to. I won't do that to you, I promise."

"How can I trust you?"

"I don't know. Perhaps time will be enough time for me to show you I can be a good person."

"Do you think you can be a good person?"

"I do. I think if I had help, if someone helped me, lead me in the right direction and gave me a reason to be good."

"Do you think I will be enough?"

"We won't know until we try. We have had an interesting start. This is not normal. You are sympathising with me, a wanted kidnapper, and I have just lost my licenses to practise medicine, rightly so too. What I did to Lucy all these years was bad. It was a game, and I had no right to play with her, her life, and her marriage, it was just..."

"Control?"

"Yes."

"I want you to go and put an end to this."

"Can I come back?"

"Yes, I would like you to come back. I would like to explore what this thing is, to explore why I feel the way I do about you, why am I so drawn to you. Is it because you are dangerous? I don't know, but right now you need to go, check on Tom, and get him home."

"Yes."

ISABEL

Izzy hung up the phone, exasperated. "He said he would look into it."

"Well, that is helpful," said Lucy.

"Is it hell helpful? They should scream around there with sirens blazing. Tom could need help! That nutter has him imprisoned, and he could be there."

"Mum, like you have said yourself, what if she is not keeping him prisoner?"

"What do you mean?"

"Oh my god mum, don't be vague now, you know what I mean, what if he has left me and is just with her, what if he has left me? Properly, not just an affair now, but Tom may have left me. Alone."

"Don't you want to find out for sure, love?" Izzy placed a hand on Lucy's shoulder.

"Yes and no. And yes, to be honest, if he leaves me then it is okay, because I am not sure how I will get past this, how we will get past this. I have so much resentment building up inside of me, not just towards Sam but towards him, and I feel guilty about that knowing that he was manipulated too, but I feel he was a little responsible; that if he had been a little more patient, understanding, and helpful even then none of this would have happened to us. I just don't know, Mum."

"Of course, you don't know, Lucy, my lovely girl. You are hurt and confused by those that are trusted and closest to you. It is going to take a lot of sorting out in your own mind. You must have a thousand questions and no answers. You may never have answers. Are you prepared for that?"

"Yes, I think so, I don't know. Like I said, I am angry, mixed up, and confused. I want to know why Tom allowed this to happen. I blame him, as hard as I am trying not to. He still cheated on me. That hurts the most. The rest I can excuse as Sam's manipulation, but not the cheating. That remains solely on his shoulders. He slept with her. God knows how many times. That was no accident or misunderstanding. I do not know how to get past that."

"But you need to. One way or the other, Lucy, you must move forward. I know that this is very painful and confusing for you, but we need to look at this methodically."

"Yes, but where do we start?"

"Step one, pen, paper and coffee!" cheered Izzy, trying to lighten the mood.

"Dome?"

They took a seat. Izzy pulled a pen and notebook from her bag while Lucy ordered them two large cappuccinos and two slabs of carrot cake with extra cream for Izzy.

Lucy put number seventy-two on the table and slid into the seat across from her mother.

"I like a booth," said Lucy.

"Do you think you will leave Tom?" asked Izzy.

"Wow, Mum, just come right out with it." Lucy looked at her hands on the table.

"Sorry, Lucy, but it is what we are both thinking."

"Not that easy. Where is he? What if he is hurt, dead, being held against his will? Part of us is assuming that he has just run off with Sam, and that is the end of it. I will collect our kids from his parents when they get back from holiday, join parents without partners, and go on with my life wondering if the next knock on the door is Tom wanting to come back into our lives, my life, our children's lives..." She let out a heavy sigh.

"But it is too late, because you have already married some rich, gorgeous man that treats you like a queen, loves the kids, cooks amazingly, and is a wonderful lover!"

"Mum! Remember, we don't know that Tom has left. He hasn't contacted work or me, and while he is a complete and utter arsehole for cheating on me, until I know for sure that he is not hurt or worse, I will not indulge in fantasies about my future husband."

"It is fun though, right?" asked Izzy.

"Mum, I don't know what I am going to do. I want to talk to him, to understand, and, more importantly, look him in the eye, have him look me in the eye. I need to know if we have any feeling left for the other. A relationship audit, if you will. Only then will I decide."

"Alright, whatever you decide, I am here for you."

"Thank you!"

The coffee and cake arrived, and they ate between taking notes. When the cake was finished, Izzy read through her notes:

"Step one: we need to find Sam and or Tom, well, definitely Tom. It is not our job to find Sam. Let the police deal with her. Although, I am sure you have some questions, Lucy, like what the fuck she thought she was doing!"

"She would only give me a pile of bullshit, Mum. Not much that girl ever told me was true. Everything is a game to her, a win-at-all costs game. I never understood what it was, and it was why I kept falling for her."

"It is your nature, Lucy. You want to believe that people mean well, that they intend to do their best, that they mean you no harm or ill will. You have been the same your whole life. It is one of the many things about you that makes you beautiful."

"I think you are referring to my gullibility, Mum."

"No, sweet Lucy, I am talking about your good heart. Do not think yourself the fool for loving people. Don't let all this shit turn you hard. It is not worth changing who you are because of the actions of others, but do not fall for their shit again either! Now, where could

Tom and or Sam be?"

"Yes, back on topic."

"Well." Izzy leaned forward across the table. "There was no sign of anyone being at the house, the grandparents' house."

"Why are you whispering?"

"Because the walls have ears. Maybe we should not be letting on out loud that we were there. It was breaking and entering, you know, and it is just our luck that you and I end up in jail, Tom and Sam get the kids, and I lose any chance of a future house sitting gig because of a criminal record."

"Shhh, Mum. You are winding yourself up again," Lucy

said. "Yes, they were not there, and we know there is a warehouse in Fremantle. I think it is time we went on that scooter tour of the city."

"What! This is hardly time for messing around, Lucy."

"We can't take my car, and with helmets on we won't be so recognisable."

"Oh, I understand. Hire a scooter, ride around incognito. I like the way you think, except I have never ridden a scooter before."

"Neither have I, but it can't be that hard if they let anyone do it."

TOM

She pushed hard against the weight of the door. Through the crack in the door, Sam could see his blood stained arm. "Tom!" she yelled.

He was the dead weight against the door. She had to use all her body weight, to edge the door open far enough to squeeze through, slicing her torso on the lock latch protruding from the door. "Tom," she yelled, kneeling beside him.

She searched his body; he was wet and sticky with the blood that oozed from his wound.

"What the hell happened?" She slapped his face. "Tom! Tom, can you hear me?"

Kicking off her shoes, she hitched him up under the arms and manoeuvred him away from the door, resting in the hallway near the bedroom. She left to collect blankets and pillows from the bedroom and first aid supplies from the bathroom. The tablets on the bathroom counter confirmed what had happened. He had been harvested. Organ theft was something that she has not seen for a long time, not since her mother died.

Sam checked his vitals. He had lost a lot of blood and his pressure was low, but there was no sign of infection yet. Sam made a makeshift bed for him in the hall, cleaned up his wound, and re-attached a drip to his arm. Sam did her best to make him warm and comfortable but he couldn't be kept on the floor. She pulled the phone from her back pocket, ran through the list of contacts. There was no one to call.

She left him, locking the door behind her. It took her ten minutes to drive the distance to Toni's house. There was no police car, so maybe she was not trying to trick her into confessing everything before going to the police. She had to trust someone now. Sam was tired of carrying all of this around with her.

"You're back?" Toni looked up from the sink full of dishes she was washing.

"Yes, I hope that is okay." Sam kissed her cheek. "I need your help."

"What is wrong?"

"It is probably better I show you. You were a nurse, right?"

"Yes. What happened, is Tom hurt?"

"I didn't hurt him, but yes, something has happened."

"Should I bring my first aid kit?"

"No, just you. I need you to help me. Please."

"Yes, of course, Sam. I said that I was here for you, and I meant it."

They did not talk on the trip, nor when the roller door to the warehouse lifted to let their car inside the warehouse, nor when Toni followed Sam through a labyrinth of corridors toward the centre of the building.

"Oh my god, that is a house, an everyday out on the street house. Is this your house?"

"No, yes, I guess it is now. It used to be a transition

house, and I had it remodelled inside to look exactly like mine."

"A transition house? What, dare I ask, is a transition house?"

"Migrants always had to pay a fee to the mob when they came here. If they had money, jewels, talents, that was easy, but sometimes people paid in flesh."

"You mean it's a brothel?"

"No, the brothel is in Northbridge; no, this is an actual flesh depository, organ donations, for rich Asians and others that can pay. Only what the person doesn't need themselves, of course."

"Of course. You mean they could buy their way into Australia with a kidney?"

"Yes, well, that is how it used to be. This whole place was shut down in 2006."

"Raided?"

"No, the family just stopped working it when my grandad died, left it be. Not more migrants, no need for this operation."

"And the house?"

"I started to have it renovated last year. There are certain trades in the system that remember my family and feel indebted, so they are happy to keep quiet. Or so I thought."

Sam opened the front door wide and let Toni see inside before stepping through the threshold.

"Wow, this place is beautiful—apart from the body, Sam!"

"It is okay, Toni, it is not a body, it is Tom. Something

has happened, and I need you to help me get him onto a bed and take care of him, please, while I sort out this mess."

Toni stood over him. "What happened?"

"I think he has been harvested. I don't know who by, but I swear I had nothing to do with it. I didn't want him hurt, not like this. Completely fucked with his head, yes, but not this. I was just playing a game, seeing how far I could push things. No one was meant to get hurt."

"Then why the fat man?"

"What do you mean?"

"Well, and don't misunderstand me here, but if no one was meant to get hurt, why did you send the fat man to rape me?"

"Rape you, yes, not to kill you. He has been with women I have set up for him before. He likes it. It is a fetish he has, but he wouldn't kill you."

"Rape is pretty fucking serious, Sam, brutal even."

"Is it?"

"Yes!"

"I guess I never really gave it much thought. I am sorry then, and I am glad that he didn't hurt you. Do you hate me?" asked Sam.

"A little, but I am more intrigued by you and more so about the effect that you are having on me. I do not really understand it, and I know that there is no logic to it. I feel bound to you."

"Then grab his feet, please."

"Where are we taking him?"

"Just into that room there."

Toni walked the few feet to the bedroom door and looks in. "We can't put him on that bed without cleaning it up. The old blood will turn rotten fast."

"Good point. Pull the bedding off, and I will fetch some new ones."

When she returned, Toni already had the old ones soaking in the bath in the en suite.

"Really?" said Sam. "I was going to throw those out."

"Really? Interesting rubbish you have there, miss?"

"See your point. Come on, let's get him in here."

Sam took a hold under Tom's shoulders and Toni took his feet and together they shuffled him back onto the bed. "Who would do this to him?" asked Toni.

"I don't know, but I have an idea about who knew that he was here. I should go pay him a visit."

"Why? What good would it do? The kidney would be contaminated or in another soul by now. What you need to do now is to make sure that Tom pulls through. You need to find a way of getting some antibiotics into him fast. Who knows what infections he has been exposed to?"

"There are tablets in the bathroom."

"It won't be enough. Any idea where we can get some intravenous antibiotics from? He is going to need more than what was left. I don't think whoever did this had any intention of him surviving," said Toni.

UNDERCOVER

"A side car? Really? I have been relegated to a sidecar?" said Izzy.

"Get in, Mum, it is your own fault for not updating your driver's license. Now put your helmet on and hold tight. This is going to be scary." Lucy pulled out into the stream of traffic. They had prepared a map of warehouses around Fremantle. They would have to search everyone to find the one that belonged to the Halong family.

Up and down the streets they went, convinced that the place they were looking for would be deserted; there couldn't be a people-smuggling ring out in plain sight. Up and down the streets they combed, peering into one warehouse after the other.

At five o'clock, Izzy got a call. She hung up briskly. "We have to take the scooter back. They are closing soon."

"Shit, we found nothing," said Lucy.

They head back to Lucy's house for a shower and a think. The bell rang as soon as they closed the door.

"Hello, Sergeant Leopold," said Lucy.

"Ladies, I was wondering if we could sit down and have a chat."

"Sure, what is this about?" asked Izzy.

"Mum, what do you think thisis about?Please, sergeant, take a seat, and I will put some coffee on."

He sat down on a stool at the island bench, and Izzy took up the seat next to him.

"How much," he began, "do you know about Sam Halong's family and family connections?"

"Not much," said Izzy.

"I know a little." Lucy said, looking at her mother. "I know her dad was a little shady, but I think her grandparents were on the straight and narrow. They were very protective of her, always insisting that she do the right thing at school, study hard, determined that she was going to be a doctor. They put a lot of pressure on her to perform well on everything she did."

"We believe that they were prominent players in an immigration racket that was running rampant throughout Australia throughout 2000 to 2010. We lost track of the key players around 2005, but then Sam's grandfather showed up in our investigation and rang alarm bells," said Sergeant Leopold.

"What do you mean, shows up? He died in 2006," said Lucy.

"Yes, he did, and no, he has not risen from the dead. Just his image and prints. We have been searching though Sam's family home and found some interesting documents relating to the illegal activity we were chasing back then. It's a cold case now, but we will reopen it and see where it leads us, and if your friend Sam has had any connection with it."

"Meanwhile," Izzy interjected, "what about my son-in-law? Any signs of him yet?"

"The problem we have, even with the message you

received from work, is there is no actual evidence that Tom has disappeared. Given the circumstances of everything that has gone on without further evidence, it could very well be that Sam and Tom have absconded together. I am sorry, I really am."

"That is not very helpful," said Izzy.

"I know, and I am sorry. Are you really convinced that something has happened to Tom other than he had been blinded with lust and manipulated into leaving you for this woman?"

"I would like to think that Tom would not just leave me like that, without a word," said Lucy.

"Yes, I get you deserve better, far better than to find out your best friend has manipulated you into an illness and your husband has been sleeping with her all this time. He must be carrying a lot of shame and guilt. Can you imagine? It all must weigh heavily on him."

"I hope it does," Izzy agreed.

"Mum, that is not helpful. What am I supposed to do, sergeant, go on with life as normal? Our kids are due home next week with Tom's parents; what am I supposed to tell them? Hey, kids, hey, parents, well, while you were gone, I had a breakdown, found out Aunty Sam was making me ill, and yes, your father has run away? That is not good enough. What am I supposed to do?"

"Honestly, I don't know. We have a watch on all his accounts, and he doesn't have his passport, so we have established that he is in the country. The hospitals report all John Does, and he has not shown up there. All we can do is wait and hope he comes home safely."

"I will walk you to the door, sergeant." Izzy led him to the door.

"Thank you for dropping by, checking up on her, but she is not the one that you need to be monitoring. I have been with her all day. You need to find Sam and Tom and this thing, whatever it is, needs to be finished."

Yes, it does, and I really am sorry. I wish that there was more I could do."

"Me too. Goodnight, sergeant."

TOM

"Can you stay with him and I will find some intravenous medication?" asked Sam.

"Me? Are you mad? What if he wakes up? Who am I supposed to be Florence Nightingale?"

"Well, you are a nurse," said Sam.

"You know what I mean," said Toni.

"Look, I understand you never signed up for this. I am sorry if this is hard. You can leave, leave now, and I will never bother you again, but I am worried and scared and I don't know what to do. If he gets an infection and dies, then they are going to blame me for murder."

"Why don't we call an ambulance, and they can take him," said Toni.

"Oh my god, what a great idea, and then they will find this place, realise that an illegal operation has been carried out here, search the premises, find out a whole plethora of dirty family secrets to air out on a Today and Tonight news show and drag my family name through the mud when the one thing I had up to now managed not to do was destroy my family name."

"Really? You don't realise that you have been all over the new as the puppet master shrink?"

"Have I? I never realised."

"What do we do, Sam?"

"You go, you are a nurse, you know your way around a hospital."

"No," said Toni. "I won't do it."

"Then let me go and hide if he wakes up. He won't remember anything but the pain if he wakes up now," said Sam.

"Okay, but hurry, this whole thing is giving me the creeps."

"Look, I will be fast, I promise, but when I get back, you should go home. Let me take care of him, of this mess, and when everything has settled down, then we can take up where we left off."

"Holy shit, are seriously dumping me in the middle of all this?"

"Dumping you? No! I am just trying to protect you."

"It sounds an awful lot like it is not you, it is just a bad time for me right now speech, and holy fuck, if there is one thing you need right now it is a friend. Hurry up before I change my mind, see sense, and leave your pathetic arse," said Toni.

LUCY

"That was not helpful. What do we do now, Mum? I mean, seriously, I keep asking, and I know that none of us know what the answer is right now, but what am I supposed to do?" asked Lucy.

"Put down that wine glass, get dressed up to play ninja, and let's case this city," said Izzy.

It was three in the morning and they were already four hours into their warehouse search.

"It has to be here." Lucy pointed at a map, close to port and the town. "It wouldn't make sense to have it too far away, but it would have to be hidden enough to disguise any movement. There is a warehouse right behind the hospital here. It is not big, but they were not storing cargo, they were storing people, and people do not need an enormous amount of space when they are in hiding."

"Well, it is worth a try, but after this one, we are heading home. I need to rest without a bike seat between my legs. We can rent a scooter in the morning," said Izzy.

"Come on then, Google says it will only take us fifteen minutes to ride," said Lucy.

As they edged around the last corner, they saw Sam come out of the roller door and head over to the rear of the hospital.

"What the... where is she going? I am going to call the sergeant," said Lucy.

"No." Isabel pushed Lucy's hand away from the phone. "We still don't know where Tom is, what he is up to, or if he is captured or absconded."

"Right, I would rather catch him out without an audience. Let him explain himself without the protection of the force around him," Lucy agreed.

They hid their bicycles, but there was no moving the roller door Sam controlled with a remote controller. It looked old and rusty on the outside, but it was double bolted stainless steel.

They found a fire exit ladder. Lucy boosted Izzy up to reach the bottom rung and pull it down, then both climbed up to the first landing and pulled the ladder back through. They peered through the street-grimed window into the darkness.

"I can't see anything," said Lucy.

Lucy tried the window; it gave a little, and she shunts it up hard.

"Well, let us get a better look," said Lucy.

"At what? It is pitch black in there," said Izzy.

"Do you want to stay here and keep watch, or would you like to come in?"

"I think I would rather stay exactly where you are, dear daughter."

Step by step they inched their way through the darkness, listening to the sound of their own breath and the light shuffle of their footsteps. They rounded a corner and saw a light.

"Mum, look," Lucy whispered.

"What the hell is that? It looks like a house, it looks like Sam's house."

"She is so bizarre. This day just keeps getting weirder. Let us get a closer look," said Izzy.

"Come on..."

They crept in the darkness towards the one lighted window and peeped inside. Crouching under the window, Lucy and Izzy could see into the room.

"That was Tom on the bed! Is he alive? I think there was a drip," said Izzy.

"There was a woman there too," Lucy returned.

"Could she be a nurse?"

"What does he need a nurse for, Mum, is he hurt?"

"You saw as much as I did. Let's do a lap of the house and see if anyone else is home." Lucy takes another peek through the window.

"Holy shit, Mum, I know that woman, that is Tom's parents' pet sitter!"

"Fucking Sam has her finger in everything. It is just not fair." Izzy looked through the glass.

"I think we can take her. Let's check out the rest of the house first to make sure that we won't be dealing with any other nasty surprises."

Lucy and Izzy circled around the house, looking inside each of the windows, trying to see if there was anyone else at the house. The rest of the house was in darkness; all they knew was that there was just the pet sitter, Toni, and Tom in the house.

"What do you want to do?" asked Izzy.

"We should just go in and confront her. She is just a pet sitter. What can she do? She has no weapons, nothing, and Tom is just lying near dead on the bed, connected to a drip."

"What if she has a weapon?" asked Izzy.

"I don't think she has a weapon, Mum."

"Okay, then let's do it, let's go in."

They went around to the front door. It was locked, and there was no other door, so they circled the house again, this time trying all the windows, but there was no way in. The entire house was double glazed and tightly shut.

"We could just smash a window," said Izzy.

Lucy rolled her eyes at her mother and walked up to the front door and knocked hard.

"Oh my god, did you forget your key?" came a voice from inside.

"She thinks it is Sam," whispered Izzy.

The door opened and there was Toni standing there gob smacked, mouth open.

"Who are you?" Toni asked.

Lucy stepped into the light. "I know who you are. What are you doing here? What are you doing with my Tom?"

"I um, um," Toni stuttered.

"Let us in." Izzy tried to barge in, but Toni was strong and pushed them back.

"You can't come in. Sam is not here."

"We don't want to see Sam, we want to see Tom. What is wrong with him? Why is he on a drip? What has she done to him?"

"I don't know, I can't tell you. What are you even doing here? How did you even find this place?"

"No, I will ask the questions. What are you doing here?" said Lucy.

"I can't tell you anything, other than I am helping Sam."

"Helping Sam with what? Whatever is going on in here is not right. That is my husband in there, and I have every right to go in and speak to him."

"I am sorry, but you can't even speak to him; he is unconscious."

"Then I have every right to find out why. Let me through." Lucy pushed hard past Toni, and this time she let her in. Izzy chested up to Toni. "Seriously? I am coming in too."

Toni stood aside. This was not her fight, and as much as she would like a relationship with Sam or she thought she wanted a relationship with Sam, or something with Sam, she wasn't quite sure what she wanted with Sam. Maybe she had just been so bored with her life that this little bit of danger, this excitement, enticed her into having a relationship that she really was not interested in... or was she? She didn't know. All she knew was that this was not her fight. She followed them into the bedroom, ready to come clean with what she knew.

"We think he has been harvested," Toni said.

"Harvested? What the hell does that mean," said Izzy.

"His organs, probably his kidney, has been stolen," explained Toni.

"What, Sam had someone steal his kidney?" asked Lucy.

"No, it was not Sam," said Toni.

"She is a liar, how do you know that it wasn't her?" said Izzy.

"No," insisted Toni, "in this case I think she is telling the truth. She is not lying. She doesn't know who it was. She was with me when it happened. She is not lying."

"She is manipulating you the same way she did me, and Tom and everyone else in her entire life," said Lucy.

"No, I don't think so. She told me about what she did to you, among others. I think this time is different. This time she has set herself up into a corner and she cannot get out of it. She has gone to get him some medicine, antibiotics, morphine for his pain," said Toni.

"Has she gone to steal it?" asked Izzy.

"Yes, to help Tom. She is putting herself at risk to help him. She doesn't want to hurt Tom. She didn't want to hurt you, Lucy," said Toni.

"Don't talk to me. You do not know me, and you do not know what she did to me. All you know is what she told you, what you have seen. And I can guarantee that all you have seen is a mask, a charade. You don't know Sam any better than I do," said Lucy.

"You are probably, right, I don't think that even Sam knows Sam. What happened to her? Why is she the way she is?" asked Toni.

Lucy looked to the ground and shrugged her shoulders. Izzy looked up and said, "No one knows. Some people are born good natured, other people bad; some walk the border between good and bad, and some fall over into bad. Sam was brought up to believe that she was brought up to walk on the good side, but there was something about her father's influence that kept dragging her back to the dark side. Sam has been doing bad things from a young age. She was a manipulative little bitch at school, and it never changed. I don't know how Lucy stayed friends with her," said Izzy.

"No, me either," came Sam's voice from the doorway. "Nice, old friends gathering to reminisce about old times. I thought my ears were getting hot," said Sam, joining the group.

"What have you done to him, Sam? What the hell have you done?" asked Lucy.

"I think it was the fat man. He has been involved in organ harvesting for a long time."

"That man is no surgeon," said Lucy.

"I never said that he was a surgeon, I said organ harvester, there is a difference. They are taught to only do one thing, they never give a guarantee that their gardens will make it. I think we have to take him to the hospital," said Sam.

"You think? You think we have to take him to the hospital? The butcher has attacked my husband, pulled god knows what organs out of him, and you think that we have to take him to the hospital? Really? Mum, call the police," said Lucy.

"Yes, call the police, but first we need to get Tom to the hospital. He has a fever. I can't get to the medication because everything is locked up and there is security everywhere. If they arrest me now, they will never find him. I am not giving this place up to the police," said Sam.

"You have run out of choices, Sam. You don't get a say

in this. You stole my husband, you drugged me, god knows what you have done to Toni, you are a liar, a cheater, where do you get off thinking that you have choices?"

"This is not about me, Lucy, this is about my grandparents. This was their place, and I am not having the police go through this. I am not having their legacy destroyed."

"You have already destroyed their name," said Lucy.

"What do you think is going to happen now?" asked Toni.

"We can take Tom to the hospital, take him to the emergency department. Let me get out of this house, lock it up and secure it. You know no one even knows that this house is here. This place has gone untouched for decades. Let it sit, just let it lie. There is nothing here that can convict me that can hurt you or me. Nothing here can convict me; please let it sit undisturbed," said Sam.

"Just how long do you think it is going to stand here for?" said Izzy.

"Until I die and beyond. This town will build itself up and tear itself down and build itself up and no one will give a second look to this place. It is heritage listed and untouchable," said Sam.

"You had this place heritage listed?" asked Izzy.

"I have friends and ways of getting things done, so no one will touch it. Please take Tom out of here, he needs help," said Sam.

Tom let out a groan that distracted them.

"He is waking up, and when he does, the pain will be unbearable. He needs to be put into an induced coma until they can operate and fix up whatever damage has been done," said Toni.

"I don't like this." Izzy looked to her daughter. "But first things first, he needs medical attention. Let's sort Tom out, make sure he is okay. Let's keep him alive because you cannot be angry at a ghost for the rest of your life. When he is better you can kill him, hurt him, give him a piece of your mind, let him squirm while you find out what the fuck he thought he was doing."

"What about the police?" asked Lucy.

"The police can chase her. We will help them find her."

Together they put Tom in grandfather's wheelchair. Lucy wheeled Tom through the warehouse, across the courtyard, out of the warehouse, through an alley, and across a carpark into the emergency department of Fremantle Hospital. Izzy got a triage nurse to come out and look at Tom, and immediately he was taken into hospital and the police were called. Izzy requested they ask for Sergeant Leopold, and he arrived shortly afterward to question them while Tom was undergoing reparative surgery.

"Where did you find him?" he asked.

"We found him in a warehouse; where is not important," said Lucy. They explained the story of the fat man, as Sam had told them. They told him everything except the location of the warehouse where they found Sam.

He warned them both that because of their refusal to tell him everything about Sam that if Tom died, they could be held accountable for his death.

"You are telling me if Tom doesn't make it, you could

charge us as accessories to his murder, when we are the reason that he is here. You did nothing to find him. I found him. My mother and I found him while you did nothing. We looked into Sam's affairs. We searched every damn warehouse in Fremantle on a bicycle. You did nothing to find my husband."

"Just saying, it is the law. I have to tell you what the law is. That is my job," said Sergeant Leopold.

"It is not fair," said Lucy.

"No, it is not fair, Lucy, and I am sorry, but if you do not tell us, I can't help you. We need to find Sam."

"You will. She will turn herself in tomorrow morning," said Isabel.

"Well, that is going to be a long wait."

"No, she will, I am sure or it," said Lucy.

"You sure?" asked the sergeant.

"No. But do you really think that you are ever going to find her if she doesn't?"

"No, probably not. To be honest, she is not a top priority on our to do list."

"Who is?"

"Drunks are far more profitable."

"That doesn't help us any, does it," said Izzy.

THE AWAKENING

After seven hours of surgery, Tom was left in intensive care alone with his wife. It was as cold as her mood towards him. She did not know how he was going to be when he woke up. She did not know how she was going to feel towards him. She had to wait.

Outside her mum paced up and down in the waiting room, waiting for her daughter, ready to take her in whatever direction she turned.

It was several days before Tom was sitting up eating and drinking and able to talk, and they edged around the issues that hung in the air like a pendulum blade swinging over their heads: where was this relationship going to go?

Neither knew. He watched her as she shuffled around the room, keeping herself busy, adjusting his curtains, his magazines, and rearranging his fruit. He loved her—he didn't love Sam, he loved Lucy. But he knew he did not deserve her. When he was asleep, she listened to the sound of him snoring, reminisced about the sound of him eating, and wondered if she really needed it all. There were quiet moments when he slept, when she wondered what life without Tom would look like, what would a life without Sam look like. Could she ever really be separated from one or the other while one of them still existed in her life?

"Why did you do it, Tom?"

"I was lonely," he said.

"Why? I was still there, every day, we were still together. Why did you sleep with Sam?"

"She kept coming on to me."

"How is that an excuse? Did you just accidentally fuck her? Repeatedly?"

"I guess, I knew Sam. We spent a lot of time together, there was a familiarity there, she was close to you."

"Yes, she was close to me, she was my doctor and my best friend... supposedly. You were not supposed to sleep with my best friend."

"Sorry, I do not know how else to say it, what else to say. I am sorry. Can you forgive me?"

"No. I don't know. I look at you, I watch you sleeping, and I just want to smash your face in. You slept with my best friend. I don't how to forgive that."

"Should we go to counselling?" Tom asked.

"Counselling? You fucked my best friend. Repeatedly; my best friend, who drugged me, betrayed me, manipulated me. Don't you see she did that because you wanted her too? I went to see Sam as a doctor because of you, because of your selfishness. I have thought a lot this week about your greed, your selfishness, your immaturity, your pathetic-ness; your what about me, is what led to all this! You made me vulnerable when you should have showed up for me, when you should have supported me. You made me vulnerable, and now I have to forgive you and again you have to take something from me, and again you weaken me, you make me vulnerable. Where were you? You were supposed to be my husband. You were supposed to be the one that I look up to. That holds me up when I am in need. The one that in the quiet moments in the middle of the night wraps his arms around me and says, "I love you". Not, what are you going to do for me? What have you done for me lately? I am going to go and find it elsewhere. Oh, my dick is so alone! No! that is not how you love people. In the dark of the night or the light of the day, it is supposed to be you that holds me. You never helped with the babies, you never altered your life. You wanted a family too, but you did nothing but walk out of that door."

"What are you saying, Lucy? Are you saying that we are finished?"

"I might be, yes, I might be. I am sorry the fat man attacked you, you will never get your kidney back."

"I will never get you back either, will I?"

"No. I just can't be a part of this relationship. I don't see in what universe I can still be your wife. How can I ever trust you, or even want to be with you? I do not see how that can happen. You are used, scarred, you already left me. The minute you stuck your dick in that woman, you left me. I am going to see your mum. I will pick up the kids, and when you get out of here, you can stay with them, your mum and dad. I am going to go home and raise my children as I always have done."

"I am sorry, Lucy. Maybe in time, do you think?"

"No, no, no, no, I do not want to entertain a thought that one day, in the future, there is forgiveness for you. You let me go so quickly, you dropped me so fast and labelled me broken and flawed. You made out that you were doing the best for me, wanted the best for me, but all you wanted was me to cook, clean, and raise your children while you went on fucking the wild thing."

The Shades of Love
Series

ALLISON

Allison's life is about to change forever. At twenty-five she is alone and free to make her own decisions. Allison is determined to follow her dreams to become a singer and a woman in charge of her own destiny.

Scott Clarke is a psychopath in the making with his sights fixed firmly on Allison. Scott threatens to turn Allison's dreams into nightmares. One by one, he eliminates those closest to her.

Will Allison escape him to live the life she dreams of with her new beau, Robert?

BALI RETREAT

Amber and Woods have had a tough year. They are partners in the force. Bali was supposed to be a holiday for them but a chance encounter on the plane over entangles them in the Balinese underworld. When Amber wakes up alone on a Kuta beach with no memory of what happened the night before, she must pull all of her resources together to find him. Can they make it home together?